Bob O'Brien is a proven author who wrote the true crime bestseller, *Young Blood: The Story of the Family Murders*, published by HarperCollins. The book was nominated for Best True Crime in the Melbourne Writers Festival.

As a homicide detective, Bob investigated some of the country's most notorious crimes, including cases of murder, drug running and violence. He methodically explained how a series of horrific murders occurred, he answered rumours about politicians and prominent people in the community who were suspected of being involved in the murders of five young men, and he and his partner arrested Bevan Spencer von Einem, one of Australia's worst murderers.

Bob left policing after thirty years to complete his doctoral dissertation about police serving as peacekeepers. He then turned his hand to running his own business. That business involved the buying and selling of water licences in Australia. He purchased water to the value of over $100 million dollars for an American investment firm.

As a business owner and a water trader, Bob wrote papers about water markets, shared his knowledge of them at national conferences and explained how they worked to visiting overseas delegations. He also co-authored academic papers about the trading of water.

First published in 2022

ISBN 978-0-6456238-0-2 (print)
ISBN 978-0-6456238-1-9 (digital)

Published by Percat Media

Front cover design by Leo Tolo, Motiv Design
Additional design and typesetting by Roy Chen

bobobrien.com.au

KHANJAR

BOB O'BRIEN

To my mentor, Peter.

*Thank you for your hard work
and your strong points of view.*

… the heavens and the earth were joined together as one united piece. Then we parted them. And we created every living thing from water.

Surah 21 al-Anbiya (The Prophets) Verse 30

PROLOGUE

PALESTINE, 2011

The young man sat on the flat roof of his grandfather's home and looked around as the sun rose from its sleep. The morning promised a beautiful, clear day. He drew in a few deep breaths as the warm rays settled on his face and he relaxed.

The streets were quiet. Traffic that serviced the metropolis known as Jerusalem was not yet moving. The young man took his eyes off the road and reached down and poked a hole with his forefinger in the black plastic surrounding the cylindrical parcel in front of him. He pulled back and the plastic ripped, revealing a prayer mat sealed from years of dust, dirt and heat. He fondled the fabric woven by his grandmother when she was a young woman. He remembered the arthritis and calluses that had developed in her small hands from years of hard work.

The colours in the wool had faded, but the strong pattern woven into the mat was clearly visible. His fingers touched and followed the design lovingly worked into the fabric. He looked around again. The streets were still silent, and he felt the peace of the morning. He slowly, carefully unwound the mat on the roof and moved to his knees.

As he knelt, he reached forward and touched the Lee Enfield .303 calibre rifle that was protected by the *sajjadat salat* and the plastic. His grandfather took the rifle from a dead British soldier many years ago. The weapon was over fifty years old, and his grandfather had rubbed machine oil on all metal parts and worked linseed oil into the wooden stock. The black metal shone like the skin of a snake in the early sunlight.

He waited patiently until a military truck stopped in front of a home two blocks away. The home, built with local stone and finished with a flat roof, was almost identical to his grandfather's house. Soldiers jumped from the rear of the truck and took their positions in the shade opposite the house. Another vehicle arrived and four men got out and moved to the front door.

The young man remembered all the things his grandfather taught him. He lay on the roof and spread his legs apart to steady his lower body. He made sure the rifle barrel did not protrude past the wall of the house, so it could not be seen from the street below. His left hand held the rifle's wooden stock underneath the barrel. With his right hand, he adjusted the rear sight on the weapon to allow for the drop of the bullet over the distance between the two homes. Then, with his right hand, he slowly pulled the rifle's bolt to the rear before firmly pushing it forward. The bolt engaged a bullet from the top of the magazine, and both slid forward. He heard the metallic click as the bolt locked the bullet in the rifle's barrel. As he carefully took aim, he pulled the weapon hard into his right shoulder so the recoil did not bruise his skin.

The young Palestinian had considered for some time whether he should aim for the person commandeering the house or a soldier. He had finally made his decision the previous night. The death needed to have maximum impact.

He sighted the rifle on the chest of his target, the Israeli soldier who appeared to be in charge. After slowly inhaling the morning air, he held his breath and squeezed the trigger. The rifle butt kicked into his shoulder, and the slug of lead sped from the barrel. He knew the bullet's deadly arc was true when the Israeli soldier fell dropping his Tavor TAR-21 assault rifle to the ground. The remaining soldiers scattered, taking cover behind their vehicle and the walls of the houses. The new settler who was commandeering the house got back into his car and drove at speed into the distance.

The young man carefully returned the rifle to its home in the prayer mat. He knew a storm was coming. The morning peace had been broken, and soldiers of the Israel Defense Forces would quickly rally and punch into the district, raiding homes of known and suspected militant Palestinians. His grandfather's house would be one of many homes searched. It had happened before.

He moved quietly to the ladder and stepped from the roof. Reaching the floor, he rolled off the last rung and saw his father staring at him with tears in his eyes. His father slapped him. Shocked, he returned his father's stare, his anger rising.

'You are not the boy I raised.'

1

Paul Shehadeh closed his laptop as EgyptAir Flight MS 985 approached John F Kennedy International Airport. He stared at the airport complex from his window seat. The airport was being modernised, but its world ranking was low compared to the big, new airports in China he had been through recently.

The Boeing Dreamliner stopped at the aerobridge at 3.15 pm, right on time. The young Palestinian engineer stood in the aisle and tried to stretch the twelve-hour flight out of his body. He was unsuccessful and hoped that reaching for his backpack in the overhead storage would loosen the knotted muscle in his shoulder.

Once off the plane, he pulled his jacket over his white shirt and headed for Customs with his cases.

Shehadeh stood behind the line printed on the floor and moved forward to the booth when the border protection officer waved him towards her. He placed his passport on the counter and the officer checked his details with those on the screen.

'Why have you come to America?' she said, after looking at the screen for ten seconds.

'I'm attending Columbia University as a research fellow for twelve months.'

There was no reply. She stamped his passport and called out, 'Next.'

He moved towards the bag checking area. People back home had warned him what to expect, so it was no surprise when an officer pointed to a line where only one person was standing. The two of them were then shown into another room.

'Please open your bags,' the border protection officer said.

Her face was expressionless. He did as she asked, and she removed the contents and checked each individual item. She held his underwear up to the light and winked to a female colleague.

'There's an unusual smell here,' she said, just loud enough for him to hear. 'We should check for explosives.'

Shehadeh stared at the officer, and his jaw tightened.

When the search was completed, an untidy mass of clothing, shoes and toiletries littered the bench.

'You can repack your bags now,' the officer said, pointing to the pile.

Shehadeh looked away, took a deep breath and forced himself to relax, repeating in his mind an old Macedonian proverb 'Every dog has its day', in an effort to control his anger.

'Thank you,' Shehadeh said, and moved to carefully fold his clothes, repack his toiletry bag and return everything to his suitcases.

Exiting the customs hall, he looked around until he saw an older, distinguished looking man holding an A3 piece of paper with the name SHEHADEH printed on it.

'Professor Marshall?'

'Hello Nasir,' he replied and gave the engineer a firm handshake. 'Welcome to America. Did you get delayed at Customs?'

'Yes, the plane was on time, but it took a while to get through the Customs checkpoint.'

'I saw when the plane landed on the arrivals board. I should've known you'd be late. Ever since 9/11, Customs at JFK have been slower than ever.' He turned towards the exit. 'Okay, let's get out of here.'

Shehadeh followed the professor to the multistorey car park and sat quietly in the car as he negotiated the roads through the airport and entered the expressway to Manhattan.

'You finished your studies in China last year?' asked the professor.

'Yes, I returned home for two months. My wife was pleased to see me and upset when I had to leave again.'

'You have children?'

'I have a son and a daughter. Unfortunately, they were sick when I left.'

'I'm sorry to hear that.'

'It happens often. The water in my country is terrible. It makes everyone unwell. That is why I'm here.'

'I see.'

The journey continued in silence until John Marshall stopped the car near an apartment building.

'This is a loading zone, Nasir, so I can't stop long. Here are the keys and some paperwork. You've got a one-bedroom apartment on the third level. It was the best I could do. The University Apartment Authority said it's a good one, and the building's close to the university. If there are any problems, contact the authority. Their details are in the paperwork.'

'Thank you, Professor. Please call me Paul. I'm adopting an English name for America. I'm hoping it will help.'

'Okay. I'll see you at my office at ten o'clock. I've marked its location on the university map. You won't have any trouble finding it.'

Shehadeh climbed the stairs to his apartment, dumped his bags and rang his wife in Palestine.

'Reem, I arrived safely. How are the children?'

'Hisham was very ill. The diarrhoea got much worse.'

'Have you taken him to the hospital?'

'We had to wait six hours, but he has a bed. He has a drip in his arm and is getting better.'

'Good, good.'

'Nasir, you must do something. Another teenager was killed in the demonstrations on the border. The water trucks can't get through when there's fighting.'

'I will, I will.'

At the end of the call, he rang his father in the West Bank. His father repeated the words he had said to him many times:

'Be strong. Your task will not be easy but persevere.'

'Yes father.'

When finished, Paul Shehadeh opened his laptop and contacted the one person he knew in America, John Tomlin at Industrial Chemical Supplies, to say he had arrived.

2

Paul Shehadeh stepped in from the cold and walked through the corridors of the Faculty of Engineering and Applied Science at Columbia University. In his head, he repeated his father's mantra: *Be strong. My task will not be easy but persevere.* After a few wrong turns, he found the door he was looking for and knocked on it.

John Marshall called with a strong voice. 'Come in.'

'Good morning, Professor.'

'Paul, did you sleep well? Is your apartment okay?'

'Yes, the university was very kind.'

'Got over the flight?

'Unfortunately, no. It takes me a few days to get over jet lag.'

'Wait till you get to my age.'

Paul fiddled with his notes, wondering how to handle his first meeting with his professor. He knew Marshall was respected across the world as an expert in the desalination of seawater and was married to an American senator.

The professor interrupted his thoughts. 'You said you finished your studies in China last year?'

'Yes. It was a wonderful experience. There is so much happening there.'

'Your class starts next week. What are your plans before the semester begins?'

'I will be working on my lecture notes, but I want to visit some sites and hope to see an old colleague of my father.'

'What are you hoping to see? The Statue of Liberty? Freedom Tower? Wall Street? Don't rush. You're here for a while.'

'I'd like to visit some of New York's water infrastructure. And … perhaps you would be able to help me with this … I was wondering if I could see some of the tunnelling for the new water pipeline for the city. I understand it's progressing well. It's a big project.'

'Yes, of course, Pipeline 3. The last figure I heard was five billion dollars.'

'I was hoping to see a tunnelling machine in operation. Do you think that would be possible?'

'It might be. I have a contact who's involved with the project. Let me get back to you on that.'

'Thank you, Professor. That would be good.'

'I was also hoping to visit the new valve chamber at Van Cortlandt Park.'

'That may be a lot harder. Security is very tight. Let me make some enquiries.'

'Thank you, Professor. You are very kind.'

'Very good. Now, a quick update on your project. I've still got half an hour.'

'Well, as you know, the desal plant will be using reverse osmosis. I have been comparing the Chinese membrane with Italian and French products. The performance of the Italian membrane looks best. The French membrane is good, while the Chinese product needs some work.

'Yes, I've found that.'

'I was hoping to use the Italian membrane with French water pumps. The French company supplies pumps to their submarine program, so they're particularly good. Also, the French have a strong presence in the Middle East, so spares will be readily available. But ...'

Paul hesitated, not sure how his news would be received.

'But since the Chinese are sponsoring the project, you will be using their pumps, pipes, and membranes?'

'Yes, Professor, that's what will happen. The positive side is that Chinese engineering, especially in large construction projects, is now superior—' Shehadeh stopped himself saying 'superior to the United States'. '... superior to most countries.'

'Yes, their construction has really improved. The Three Gorges Dam project is very impressive. Did you get to visit the dam?'

'I was fortunate to get some work experience at the dam. You're right, it's an amazing piece of engineering. And with China's population so large, their pool of engineers is growing. More numbers means more talent.' Paul looked at his project notes. 'Chinese solar panels and batteries don't have the quality of American ones but are cheaper. I'm looking at American tunnel boring machines, however. I'm really looking forward to seeing a big machine in operation. I think America leads the world with its tunnelling and boring techniques. Your directional drilling is among the best in the world.'

He saw the Professor nodding knowingly.

'I don't have to tell you that, do I?' I'm sorry. I get excited when I think about getting clean water to my people.'

'Yes, we've a long history of tunnelling and boring that started with our oil industry.'

'I want to put my pipeline underground to Gaza and one day extend it to the West Bank. I'll need to protect it from the heat and even terrorist operations. For the moment, I'm not sure my project will need a tunnel boring machine. Trenching and backfill will be the solution in low lying areas.'

'You're going underground to Gaza and later extending to the West Bank?'

'Yes.'

'Where will the desalination plant be built?'

"The Chinese want to put it in the Sinai near Arish on the Mediterranean Sea.'

'In the Sinai?'

'Yes, the Chinese want it there.'

'The desalination plant for Palestine is to be built in Egypt?'

'Yes.'

'Why do the Chinese want the plant to be built in Egypt? Why not build it on the coast in Gaza ... on Palestinian soil?'

Paul Shehadeh hesitated, thinking. He looked deep into the eyes of his professor, who was old enough to be his father, then looked at the floor as his mind raced. He took a breath and continued.

'Professor, can I trust you? You know it is important to me that Palestine has a water supply independent of Israel.'

'Paul, what are you trying to say?'

Paul looked around the room struggling for words, trying to avoid a direct answer. 'China has already built a desalination plant in Gaza. But, Professor, it is tiny. It helps the local community, but it is too small for the whole of Gaza, let alone the West Bank.'

'Why don't you make the current desalination plant bigger to cater for more people?'

'I'm not sure. The Chinese would have their reasons.'

John Marshall frowned. He rose slowly from his chair and came over to place his hand on Paul's shoulder. 'Thank you. That's enough for today. Let's continue with weekly meetings. Before the next one, send me your findings comparing the different qualities of French, Italian and Chinese membranes used for the desalination of sea water.'

Shehadeh left the office and walked into the cold air. His thoughts weighed on him. It wasn't the start he wanted. He must be more careful if he wanted American support for his project to get water to Palestine.

3

Paul Shehadeh lifted his collar as the breeze whipped his windcheater. He ignored the beauty and size of the park and walked past the launching ramp for the rowing boats on the edge of Central Park Lake and continued towards Loeb Boathouse. He was worried that his presence at the university was causing concern. He revealed more information than he intended at his first meeting with Professor Marshall. Important matters he had omitted from his application for entry into Columbia were coming to light. He had hoped their omission would be missed or overlooked because his project would be seen to be important for humanitarian reasons.

Shehadeh forced his concerns from his mind as he neared the restaurant. He entered and was shown to a table overlooking the cold waters. John Tomlin stood as he approached.

Tomlin had employed Paul's father as an interpreter when he was working in Lebanon. Shehadeh did not know what the work involved, but Tomlin and his father had kept in touch, emailing at least once a year. When Paul made contact, Tomlin suggested they meet at the restaurant.

'This is a bit different from the Middle East, isn't it Nasir?' said Tomlin. It was a comment more than a question.

'Yes, it is. Please call me Paul. I am using that name while I am in America.'

'Sure thing.'

'Thank you for inviting me here. I wanted to see the famous lake. I was hoping to take a photograph of the gondola on the water for home, but it's not there.'

'Wrong time of year. Central Park is beautiful in summer, with the gondola and boats on the lake, but winter can still be nice. The park is a lovely area to walk or jog around, but it's better in summer.'

'Water for boating. It is nothing like home. There's not enough water for bathing let alone boating.'

'Are you drinking? I'm ordering a glass of red wine.'

'Pepsi. Thank you.'

'How is your father?' Tomlin asked.

'He is well. He sends his best wishes. He says that you are a good man.'

'Thank you. I understand he has retired?'

'He finished last year, after fifty years in the classroom. He was getting tired and said it was time for younger teachers.'

Their small talk continued until their food arrived.

'My father was a bit vague when I asked how he knew you.'

Tomlin smiled. 'I worked for the Central Intelligence Agency. I was based in Afghanistan. There wasn't much fighting going on in the early days, but we were trying to disrupt the growing of opium poppy.'

Shehadeh did not say anything.

'It was the time of sex, drugs, and rock and roll in the States. Too many of our young people and Vietnam vets were getting into heroin, so the CIA got involved in Afghanistan. Unfortunately, it was one of the few ways farmers could make money and, naturally, the people on the land began to dislike us.'

'Perhaps the problem was western lifestyle, not the growing of poppies, which poor farmers have cultivated for thousands of years.'

Tomlin sighed. 'You're right. Anyway, it was the beginning of our involvement in the country. I had to pop over to Lebanon. We believed opium extract was being converted to heroin there before being shipped to America. I needed an interpreter, and your father spoke three languages.'

'But now you are in the chemical business?'

Tomlin was finishing his food. 'I left the agency twelve years ago. I manage a business that supplies bulk product to the water treatment industry. In fact, I have a meeting with my boss here in half an hour.'

Tomlin took a drink of water. 'So, you are lecturing at Columbia. Very impressive.'

'Thank you. I am very pleased to be in America. I want to learn more about tunnelling techniques used here.'

Shehadeh spent the next twenty minutes outlining his project with the Chinese. After the reaction from his supervising professor, however, he did not say that the plant was to be built in the Sinai.

'The Chinese are moving fast. The agency was always concerned about the growth of China, I didn't think that they would get involved in the Middle East. It's a real melting pot.'

As they drank their coffees, the conversation moved to water infrastructure in America.

'I'm trying to visit the new valve chamber and filtration plant at Van Cortlandt Park. It is amazing what America has done there.'

'We supply chemicals to the filtration plant there,' said Tomlin. 'It is impressive.'

'Could you help me visit the site?'

John Tomlin thought for a moment. 'Well, we do have a large shipment of chemicals going there in a little while. We might be able to arrange something.'

Shehadeh smiled. 'That would be fantastic.'

As the conversation wound up, a man approached their table. Tomlin stood up. The man's skin was dark, but Shehadeh wasn't sure whether the colour was fake or natural.

'Richard, can I introduce you to Paul Shehadeh. He's the son of a friend of mine in the Middle East. Paul, this is Richard Moses.'

Paul stood and offered his hand. 'Pleased to meet you, Richard.'

Richard Moses took Paul's hand, but there was no warmth in his handshake.

'Paul is lecturing at Columbia for twelve months. He was telling me about a water project he is involved in.'

'Oh?'

'He's assisting the Chinese with a desalination project for Palestine. There may be some opportunities for us?'

Moses' demeanour changed. 'Really? Now that is interesting.'

He pulled out a chair and sat at the table. 'Tell me about it.'

4

Semra Bekele grabbed a spot in the middle of the minibus that was taking her and twelve other agents to the FBI Training Academy at Quantico, Virginia, for the FBI's two-day proficiency course.

'Bec, you're deep in thought,' remarked Jessica White, who was sitting next to her.

'Uh ha,' she replied still looking out the window.

The pair had worked together for two years as partners. Now, Jessica was her supervisor. They had both just received commendations for a job they worked on for a year. A parcel post bomber was driving the FBI crazy. Through hard work, Bec found a possible suspect and started surveillance on him. The surveillance team was particularly good and filmed him posting a parcel bomb. Jessica led the raid on his house and Bec tackled the bomber as he ran away, despite being unsure at the time if he was wearing an explosive vest.

Bec received the FBI Medal of Valor, and Jessica received a promotion. Now, Bec was looking for a new partner.

'Have you thought about who you would like to work with?'

Bec pursed her lips as the minibus turned into Bureau Parkway and approached the academy. 'No, not really.'

'What about Gary Peters?'

'Casanova? No, I don't want to work with a ladies' man.'

'Rodriguez?'

'He spends all his time avoiding work.'

'Marilyn Kerber?'

Bec raised her eyebrows and looked to the heavens. 'Sycophant.'

The minibus stopped in front of the gymnasium and Bec saw her old partner looking at her.

'I want an answer by next week.'

She knew Jessica was serious.

'Let me get back to you.'

The first day of the proficiency course involved physical activities: running, jumping over fences and hand to hand combat. Bec was happy competing against the guys in the fitness program. Although most of the men were stronger, she was more flexible. And she was fit. She had been athletic at school and had performed well in her FBI recruit course three years ago.

By the end of the day, an accumulation of sweat had dried on her body, leaving salty deposits on her dark skin. Bec was keen to know her overall score for the first day and went over to look as soon as they were placed on the board. Only two other agents bested her. Musa Halmat from her office in New York was one. The other agent came from the FBI office in Washington.

Bec watched as Jessica came into the gym. Her face was

red, and she was breathing heavily from the last task of the day. 'How did you go?'

'Not last, but time to lose a few pounds.'

'Wind down on the basketball court?'

'Good idea. Otherwise, I'll grab a shower and end up heading straight for the bar.'

After thirty minutes, Bec and Jessica stopped shooting hoops and grabbed their towels. As they were leaving, Bec saw Musa Halmat in the boxing ring, sparring with another agent, Martinez, from the Washington office. She knew Musa by name, but they had only ever said a passing hello. After besting her in the first day's point score, she decided to watch him in the ring.

The gym instructor called 'time' to end the round, but Martinez was slow to stop and smashed his right hand into Musa's face, breaking his nose. Blood flowed as Martinez walked back to his corner.

'Whoah,' the gym instructor called out. 'Alright, let's call it a day.'

'We have another round,' Musa said quietly but with authority. The gym instructor stared at him for a few seconds and nodded.

'Last round.'

Bec continued watching with Jessica as the two agents moved to the centre of the ring. Martinez danced on his toes, a slight smile on his face. Musa stepped close to his opponent. His jab flashed forward, just touching Martinez' face as he found his range, then his fist hissed forward striking Martinez in the right eye, removing the grin from his face. Musa followed with his right hand. The punch hit Martinez powerfully in the chest, slightly to the right of the sternum where his heart sat, and his legs buckled.

Bec's eyes widened. She knew that one more punch would put him on the canvas. But Musa stepped back and allowed his fellow agent to recover. Then, for the next one and half minutes, Musa moved forward to hit him at will, stepping back and then moving forward again. With fifteen seconds to go in the round, he moved forward one last time and smashed his right fist into the nose of Agent Martinez. It flattened and broke.

That night, Bec spoke with different agents about Musa Halmat. She learned he spent ten years in New York's police department before joining the FBI. Her colleagues said he was a good operator, and his nickname, which no-one called him to his face, was Moose.

'Why is he called Moose?' Bec asked Jessica, when she entered the recreation room. 'Is it a play on his name?'

Jessica took a sip from her hot chocolate before answering. 'I've got an idea, but I'll let you find out.'

Bec gave Jessica a questioning stare, but the only response she got was a smile.

The last test of the proficiency course was the one-and-a-half-mile run. The first group of twelve agents from the Washington office completed their run, the leaders finishing in under six minutes. The contingent from New York took their positions on the track. The bigger, heavier agents stood back allowing the faster runners to lead. Bec took her position at the front. She was surprised to see Musa, with his powerful body, stand alongside her. Normally, fast runners at that distance were much leaner. Her eyes moved to his face; his newly broken nose didn't weaken his rugged features.

The starting gun fired. Bec took off and moved to a loping rhythm. Musa followed and was behind her at the end of the first lap.

Let's see if you're still with me at the end of the next lap.

He was. Bec accelerated her pace for fifty yards and, as she expected, Musa fell behind. But she soon heard his heavy breathing again. At the start of the last lap, he was at her shoulder. With two hundred yards remaining, Musa accelerated and sprinted past. Bec was slow to react, but she was back with him when she saw him lose his rhythm. He had started his sprint too early.

Bec stayed just behind his right shoulder. Fifty yards from the finish line, she accelerated. She glimpsed him trying to respond, but he was running on empty. She pushed her head and chest forward, and arms back as she crossed the finish line in front. She wanted to finish with style.

Bec looked back to see Musa stop on the track immediately after he finished. She could see that he was spent. His head was down, and his big chest was heaving. But he remained standing, sucking air.

As she walked towards him, she was still breathing heavily. 'I thought ... you had me.'

Musa nodded and walked off. Bec stood watching him. She might have just found her new partner.

5

The early morning light poured through the windows of New York's FBI office in Federal Plaza, Manhattan. Bec looked around the open office until she found Musa, working at a desk computer in a corner, typing at speed with two fingers.

'Hi, Musa. You free?'

He continued typing for a long fifteen seconds before slowly looking up from the keyboard. 'Jessica asked if I would like to work with you.'

'That's right,' said Bec.

'Why me?'

'It seemed like a good idea at the time,' replied Bec, with a cheeky smile.

'Pretty smile. You're a real charmer.'

For a moment, Bec was speechless. The word 'charmer' had a specific meaning in the office, especially amongst the older agents. It referred to a new breed of agent who were talented at telling everyone how good they are, rather than showing their ability in the field.

'What do you mean?'

'If you want to work with me, ask me before going to our supervisor,'

'Okay. Got the message. I thought I should check with Jessica first. Perhaps, I should forget about it. My mistake.' She stood there looking at Musa, then decided to try a different tack. 'What are you working on?'

'Stolen artefacts from the Middle East. A Middle Eastern job for a Middle Eastern guy.'

Bec wasn't sure if it was his sense of humour, or if he was angry.

'What was taken?'

'A lot of items went missing from the National Museum of Iraq after we went in to remove Saddam Hussein. I'm looking for a display of daggers. The Iraqis believe they were stolen by American soldiers when they took over Baghdad. The most valuable was a matching pair of khanjars.'

'Khanjars?'

'Arabian daggers.' He took a long breath and leaned back in his chair. 'A matching pair was the most valuable. They were believed to be made for an Omani sultan and his son a couple of centuries ago.'

'Wouldn't the military police investigate that?'

'Normally, but it's got political. A Senator Donaldson pushed for the FBI to do it.'

'Why is it political?'

'You ask a lot of questions, don't you?' said Musa, looking at Bec as if deciding whether to answer. 'It appears to be organised rather than opportunistic stealing by soldiers. The media think there is a story, so the FBI was asked to look into it.'

'What are they worth?'

'Priceless, apparently. A curator at the City of New York museum said a matching pair of Arabian daggers was extremely unusual. From the information she was given from the museum in Iraq, she thought one Arabian dagger of their quality could be worth as much as a hundred thousand dollars, but she thinks this matching pair with its backstory is priceless.'

Bec raised her eyebrows and whistled.

'And because my family is from the Middle East, I got the job.'

'Any suspects?'

'The last person seen with the artefacts was a John Tomlin. He was a CIA agent gathering intelligence in Iraq and was seen taking away the artefacts for safe keeping. He lives in New Jersey and manages a chemical supply warehouse. So, I was going to speak to him to see if he can help.'

'Any photographs of the daggers?'

Musa opened his computer file and various pictures of Arabian daggers came to life. Bec stared at the matching pair. 'They remind me of home.'

'Home?'

'Ethiopia. The civil war. Mainly guns, but jiles were used. Nothing fancy like those.' Bec hesitated for a moment, deciding whether to try again. 'Why don't we work on it together. If it doesn't work out, we can go our separate ways.'

'And you tell Jessica you can't work with me?'

'No, I tell Jessica we agreed to try it for a month, that's all. She'll be okay with that.'

'Let me think about it,' replied Musa. He looked at Bec without speaking. His face frustratingly inscrutable. 'You know the daggers are cursed.'

'What do you mean?'

'They cause bad luck. A sultan owned the larger dagger and had a smaller matching one made for his son. But the little guy wanted the bigger one. So, he slit his father's throat and became sultan.

'Charming.'

'Legend has it that anyone who holds the khanjar is cursed.'

'That's ... serious.'

'I don't want to bring you bad luck,' said Musa, still with a straight face.

'Sure,' she said, shrugging her shoulders. 'Is that a yes?'

She took the hint of a nod as an affirmative and walked to Jessica White's office.

'I've just been speaking with Musa. Now I know why his nickname is Moose. He's one ornery beast.'

Jessica smiled. 'Still want to work with him?'

Bec thought about it for a while. 'Yes, I'd like to give it a go. See if it works. As you know I'm going to Canada for my annual leave to see family; can I start with Musa when I come back?'

'Okay, you're his partner for six months.'

"I said we could try it for one month.'

'Six months, and then I'll consider a change.'

'Six months it is, then. He's investigating stolen artefacts from Iraq. Should be interesting.'

6

Lucy Donaldson jumped from Professor John Marshall's car on Amsterdam Avenue.

'Thanks for the lift.'

She slammed the door and drifted towards Columbia University's engineering school, arriving early for her morning class.

She sat by herself in the lecture theatre, while most other students talked in groups of twos and threes while waiting for class to begin. When the sun moved around, the winter sunlight forced its way through the grime on the window. She removed her jacket and then closed her eyes as the sun warmed her face.

Lucy let her mind wander and waited for her Middle Eastern Studies lecturer to arrive. She had no idea why the subject was part of an engineering degree at Columbia University. She was aware of the problems in the region, and that the United States had been lured into conflict in the area. But why the United States had become involved after Britain and France long since stopped trying to impose their will on the Middle East was a mystery to her. No doubt it had something to do with oil, but now the US was producing more oil from fracking, and they would no longer need their black gold.

'Hi, anyone sitting here?'

Lucy opened her eyes to see a student standing in the aisle looking at her. She smiled.

'No, help yourself.'

'I'm Rosa,' said the young woman, as she sat down.

'Lucy.'

A man wearing a dark suit, white shirt and tie entered the room. Lucy watched as he moved to the lectern. She shifted in her seat and studied her new lecturer. He certainly didn't look like one of the traditional academics in the engineering faculty at Columbia. She might not learn much in Middle Eastern Studies, but Dr Paul Shehadeh would certainly help the time pass.

7

Paul Shehadeh shuffled his papers, linked his laptop to the projector using Bluetooth and waited for the room to fill with students. His semester lectures for engineering students at Columbia University were beginning. He wondered how committed his students would be. Middle Eastern Studies was only worth three points towards an engineering degree. It wasn't as important as the core subjects, which were valued at twelve points and would be taken more seriously by students.

The final few budding engineers entered the room. As his smart watch reached commencement time, Shehadeh looked up.

'Thank you.'

Everyone stopped talking, and most looked towards him. A few students remained on their cell phones reading or typing messages.

'I ask that iPhones be placed on silent and not used unless you're taking notes or photographing the whiteboard.'

He waited as students fiddled with their phones.

'You, at the back, have you put your iPhone on silent?'

The young man with a flattop haircut continued to text for a few more moments before lifting his head.

'Sorry,' he said, without smiling. 'You said put our iPhones on silent. I have a Samsung.'

Shehadeh stared at him. Other students in the class turned to look towards the young man. Shehadeh gave him a half smile. *Every dog has its day*, he thought before continuing. 'My name is Dr Paul Shehadeh. If you are here for Middle Eastern Studies, you are in the right room.'

Immediately, an older woman sitting in the third row looked embarrassed, gathered her backpack and left quickly without saying anything.

'If you are interested in historic architecture and the engineering associated with it, then the Middle East is relevant to you and your studies. So much engineering of the ancients is to be found there.'

'The principles of Pythagoras and discoveries of Archimedes were used throughout the Middle East well before western civilisation left its nappies behind. Their wisdom is still being applied today – in this very school and throughout America every day.'

Shehadeh praised and listed the developments of algebra, mathematics and physics in the Middle East. When several of the young men in class became restless, he knew it was time to move on.

'But ...' He paused and pointed towards the ceiling then lowered his voice. 'But, what I have said so far is not the future. Let me tell you what is currently happening and what engineering projects will occur in the Middle East. These projects, especially those linked with Chinese funding, will have an impact on all of us.'

He waited before quietly continuing.

'Who has heard of BRI – the Chinese Belt and Road Initiative?

Several students raised their hands. Shehadeh nodded at the class and then continued.

'The president of China, Xi Jinping, first mentioned this initiative in 2013, one year after he rose to power. He visited Kazakhstan and Indonesia and talked about the trade between China and the West via the old Silk Road. The old Silk Road facilitated travel and the movement of goods between China, the Middle East and Europe. These trade routes had economic foundations, but the trails created by the feet and hooves of thousands of men and animals over centuries became roads with places for overnight refuge. Many of these refuges became hotbeds of cultural, political, and religious activity. You can think of Tehran, Baghdad, Damascus, Jerusalem, Ephesus and Constantinople, which is now Istanbul. Further north, there is Almaty in Kazakhstan. But what happened to the old Silk Road? What was its fate?'

The students in the class were silent. Shehadeh waited patiently until a student finally raised his hand and spoke.

'The routes still exist, but their importance has lessened. The overland routes have been superseded by container ships coming out of China.'

'Correct. Can you tell your fellow students about the Belt and Road Initiative?'

'China is developing new trade routes based on the old Silk Road concept. China is building some seaports, as well as road and rail links in various countries.'

'Correct again.'

Shehadeh reached down and opened an app on his

laptop. Colour came to the lecture theatre screen, and the Belt and Road Initiative came alive.

A young, fair-haired woman in the fifth row raised her hand.

'Excuse me, I understand the road concept, but why use the term 'belt' for the initiative?'

'There are a variety of explanations, but the best I've heard is that the belt initiative calls for the integration of the Eurasian land mass into a cohesive economic area. As a belt supports or holds together clothing, the Chinese are looking to support a growing Eurasian region.' He looked up at the whole group. 'Now, who can tell me how much money the Chinese Government is putting into BRI?'

Different figures were thrown about – one billion, five billion, ten billion – but none of the students came close.

'Thirty billion dollars. China is using Singapore as a financial and business centre to facilitate BRI. The China Construction Bank is supplying thirty billion dollars to support Singaporean and Chinese companies investing in BRI projects.'

He went on to speak about developments in Malaysia, Bangladesh, Sri Lanka and Pakistan. When he moved on to Djibouti, on the horn of Africa, a student at the back interrupted.

'What's this to do with engineering and Middle Eastern Studies?'

Shehadeh forced himself to remain calm.

'I understand your question. It's hard to see the relevance at the moment. But, please be patient and you will soon see the connection.' He turned back to the rest of the class. 'China is becoming more involved in Africa and the

Middle East. They are spending billions of dollars, and their influence is spreading. It will impact all western nations, including America.'

He paused and took a moment to try to relax.

'Now you will see the relevance of what I have been talking about. I'm going to talk about a project where I have a role. One of the Chinese Belt and Road projects is a base on the Mediterranean in Egypt. It is the development of a seawater desalination plant in the Sinai. The plant will be built near Arish.'

A map of the Mediterranean came on the screen followed by a larger scale map of Egypt and the Sinai.

'The plant will supply water to Arish, here in the Sinai, and the Palestinian city of Rafah in the Gaza Strip. It has a budget of one billion dollars. My role is to help with the construction of the pipeline from Arish to Gaza. I'm calling my part of the project, Living Water. Perhaps someone could suggest why I chose that name.'

A dark-haired young woman put her hand up. She was sitting next to the student who'd asked a question earlier. Paul nodded to her.

'The prophet Jeremiah talks of God as the spring of living water.'

'Very good,' said Paul. 'Yes, living water is mentioned in both the Bible and the Quran.'

'Perhaps our new lecturer is planning to be the saviour of Palestinians?' said the young woman.

There was a ripple of laughter around the lecture theatre.

'To an extent, yes. The project will solve a very serious problem. And it will all be powered by green energy. The desalination plant will be powered by solar panels and wind capable of producing ninety megawatts of electricity with battery backup. In total, 250,000 solar panels with three wind turbines.

'In the next session, we will discuss other engineering projects that will change the Middle East. I will also talk about your assignment. Any questions?'

Around the room, students started closing laptops and packing their bags.

'Thank you. See you next week.'

8

'Why do we need to go to the vice president's office? Can't you tell me what's happening?' asked Paul Shehadeh, worried what a visit to her office might mean.

Professor John Marshall continued walking at a fast pace. 'As I said, she wants to have a chat about your application to attend Columbia.'

They entered the offices of the Vice President, Human Resources. The receptionist immediately ushered them through. Vice President Claire Conway was already seated with the head of the engineering school, Peter Papadopoulos. Another man, big and probably Hispanic, was also at the table. From his demeanour, Paul doubted he was from the university.

'Professor, Dr Shehadeh, take a seat, said Claire Conway. 'You both know everyone here except Tony Flores.' She looked briefly over to the big man sitting at the table. 'Tony is from the government.'

Paul nodded, wondering what part of the government he represented.

'I understand, Dr Shehadeh,' said Claire Conway, 'you have been studying in China and have applied for post-doctoral research at Columbia. It appears, however, that you have not been completely truthful in your application.'

Paul Shehadeh was surprised but quickly recovered.

'There are no lies in my application.'

The vice president responded quickly and forcefully.

'Did you say the Palestinian desalination plant was to be built in Egypt? Did you say you wanted the water pipeline to extend to the West Bank?' Her voice rose slightly in pitch as she spoke each sentence. 'Did you say you wanted to cross Israeli land to get to the West Bank? What do you call it? I call it lies by omission.'

The vice president took a breath.

'The university is unhappy that there was not full disclosure of your project when you applied to come to Columbia. You have left the university in a difficult position.'

Shehadeh tensed. 'Not as difficult as the position of my people.'

'Dr Shehadeh, your project to supply desalinated water to Palestine is an admirable one, and the university supports the concept. The university was prepared to overlook that it has Chinese funding, but building the plant in Egypt and wanting to continue the pipeline to the West Bank...' Claire Conway didn't finish. She shook her head. 'You know that means putting a pipeline across Israeli land, don't you?'

Shehadeh's anger rose. 'Of course, I know. I'm Palestinian. It is *our* land.' His voice was strained. He forced himself to take a deep breath before continuing. 'Ms Conway, I want to help my people. We don't have clean water like Americans. I'm here to let Americans know what is happening and to get support for my project. Americans don't know what is happening or they just don't care. If Americans did not have water, they would understand.

They would care.'

'Paul,' Professor Marshall said gently, 'I want to help you. I wouldn't be supervising you if I didn't. But I can't help you if you're not completely frank with the university.'

Shehadeh took another quiet breath and forced a smile. 'Professor, there were no lies in my application. Let me ask you. Would the university accept my application if I mentioned Sinai and the West Bank?'

John Marshall did not answer.

'Dr Shehadeh, I understand you are scheduled to speak about your project to Americans for Palestine next week,' said Claire Conway. 'You will cancel that talk. You will not speak of your project to anyone but Professor Marshall until the university works through the issues. Do you understand?'

'But ...' Paul Shehadeh stopped. It was no use arguing. He thought for a moment. 'Ms Conway, I applied to Columbia because your university supports research and teaching on global issues. That's why I came here. I just want to help my people.'

'Yes, yes, of course. But, Doctor Shehadeh, I stress that you are not to talk about this project until the university considers these matters. Do you understand?'

Shehadeh took a moment to weigh up his options before responding. When he had made up his mind, he said with a firm voice, 'Yes, Madam Vice President. I will do what you say.'

9

Paul Shehadeh followed a group of young undergraduates into the lecture theatre and then moved to the lectern. He watched the students chatting as they walked to the middle of the room and sat down. Paul took his laptop out of his bag and opened it up. He looked up when he realised the students had suddenly gone silent. Three young women were staring at something behind him. One of them looked over to him, and her face coloured.

Shehadeh turned around and saw for the first time what his students had noticed. 'Hadji classroom' in black capital letters shouted at him from the whiteboard. Another group of students walked in and saw the words as they were standing in one of the aisles. They muttered something and then continued to some seats towards the back of the theatre.

Shehadeh stopped and stared at his students for a few seconds. His hands formed fists for a short time, and then his fingers relaxed and opened. He moved purposefully to the lectern where he found the eraser and quietly removed the words. As he turned back to the class, a young man at the back of the room stood. He smirked at Shehadeh before moving athletically down the aisle and towards the door. Paul recognised him as the student he'd told to stop texting in class … and the author of the message on the whiteboard.

The remaining students found their seats. Most of those in groups were talking to one another; others were just looking, waiting.

'Let's get started,' said Shehadeh. 'I want to talk about your assignment. You will be required to research the engineering of any water project in the Middle East and compare it with one in America.'

He now had the attention of all the students in the class.

'You could compare the Hoover Dam, which was constructed from concrete, with the Aswan Dam on the Nile. Aswan is the world's largest embankment dam. Another project could involve comparing desalination plants in America with one in the Middle East. The largest desalination plant in America is the Calsbad plant in California, while the United Arab Emirates has three under construction.'

Some of the students appeared to be already searching the internet for the sites he'd mentioned.

'Of course, any students who present different examples might get more marks.'

The rest of the lecture was taken up discussing engineering projects. When he'd finished, two students who had spoken in his first lecture approached him as the last of the class were leaving the theatre. One of them was the fair-haired young woman who had asked a question.

'Dr Shehadeh,' she said.

Paul Shehadeh stopped packing his laptop into his backpack.

'Yes.'

'I'm sorry about the words on the whiteboard. That shouldn't have happened. I thought people at Columbia were better than that.'

Looking at this upfront young woman, it was hard to hold onto the anger he'd been feeling.

'That's very kind of you. Unfortunately, these things still happen. You are?

'Lucy Donaldson.'

'Lucy Donaldson, thank you very much.'

'Hi, I'm Rosa,' said Lucy's companion.

'Yes, I remember. Our scripture expert from the first lesson. Thank you, Rosa. Let's hope our next class is less eventful.'

Shehadeh found himself smiling as he watched the two students walk away. His anger had left him, but he wasn't sure he was ready to totally dismiss the incident.

10

Shehadeh arrived at one of the many plain doors in the university building of the engineering school and knocked. Professor John Marshall answered.

'Come in.'

'Hello, Professor. Are you free?'

'Hi Paul. Sure. Take a seat.'

Paul stepped further into a small room, with its shelves full of engineering books and student papers in piles on the floor. He noticed a small model of the Library of Celsus on a shelf opposite Professor Marshall's desk. He'd seen the magnificent structure, built in the city of Ephesus when it was part of the Roman Empire, when his father had taken him to the city's ruins as a teenager.

Paul sat in the chair opposite the professor. John Marshall was exactly what he expected prior to arriving in America: a few strands of grey blended in dark brown hair, but young looking for someone who must be in his sixties.

'Paul, what's up?'

'I had an incident in my class this morning.'

'What happened?'

'The words "Hadji Classroom" were written on the whiteboard. It upset some of my students.'

'And you?'

'I was disappointed,' said Paul, not wanting to mention his anger.

'If I remember rightly, Hadji refers to a Muslim who has made his pilgrimage to Mecca.'

'Yes.'

'You've made your pilgrimage to Mecca?'

'No, not yet. I'm hoping to after I finish the pipeline to Gaza.'

'So, it's offensive to use the word if you haven't made your pilgrimage?'

'It's more than that. American soldiers use Hadji as a nickname for people from the Middle East, in the same way they used Charlie or Gooks to describe their enemy in Vietnam. It's a slur.'

'I see.'

The professor looked away for a moment before speaking.

'Paul, I'm sorry that happened. From my experience, that sort of thing is very unusual. I've never heard of anything like it happening before. I'll mention it to the head of school.'

'I really don't want it to cause a problem for the university, or for me or my project.'

'I assure you that won't happen. Your syllabus has been approved by the school?'

'Yes.'

'Email me a copy of your program and when it was approved.'

Marshall made some notes about the incident.

'As I said, I'll have to mention it to the Head of School.'

'Are you sure? I don't want any problems.'

'It needs to be reported.' The professor placed his pen on his table. 'Alright, let's move on. How is the planning going for your pipeline from the desalination plant?'

'I'm——'

There was a knock on the professor's door. Lucy Donaldson entered but stopped abruptly.

'I'm sorry, John. You said two o'clock.'

'Come in. Yes, I did say two o'clock. Lucy, can I introduce you to Nasir Shehadeh. He likes to be called Paul. I'm supervising some research he's undertaking.'

Lucy Donaldson smiled and thrust her hand forward for a handshake. 'Yes, we've met. I'm in Dr Shehadeh's class. I'm learning all about engineering projects in the Middle East.'

'Lucy, what a surprise.'

'Well ... that is a coincidence,' said the professor. 'I'm helping Paul with his desalination project. He's looking to provide an independent water supply to Palestine. Anyway Lucy, let's talk later. Are you home tonight?'

'I'll be home about eight. I have a late class.'

'Okay, let's catch up then.'

Lucy walked over to the professor and gave him a kiss on his cheek. She smiled at Paul as she turned to leave. 'See you in class, Dr Shehadeh.'

11

Senator Debra Donaldson was taking the opportunity to sit at the breakfast table with her husband in their home in Murray Hill near midtown Manhattan. They had been married three years, and in that time they had rarely had breakfast together. Often, she would leave early for a morning meeting.

'Not hungry?' asked her husband.

She looked down at the half-eaten bacon pancake and smiled. 'Sorry, thinking about my Foreign Affairs Committee meeting this afternoon.'

She took a mouthful of pancake.

'I'm working on an initiative that I hope will improve the situation in Palestine.'

'Good luck with that.'

'Thank you, dear,' she responded, pretending to be gracious, but then shook her head. 'With so much bitterness on both sides, I'll need all the luck in the world to successfully initiate even the smallest change.'

'When's your flight to Washington?'

'Late this morning,' she said. 'And how's work?'

'The marking of papers is starting to drive me crazy.' He sipped a mouthful of coffee. 'It's time I thought of retiring.'

Lucy Donaldson entered the kitchen and grabbed a coffee. 'What about you, Lucy?' asked her mother.

'What about what?' she said sliding onto a kitchen chair.

'What classes are you doing this semester?'

'Mostly the same.' She sighed. 'But I'm starting to wonder whether I'm cut out to be an engineer. John lied to me. The math is hard work.'

'I did not.'

'Yes, you did.'

'That's enough,' said Debra. 'No games this morning, both of you.'

Lucy smiled at her stepfather. 'But I'm enjoying Middle Eastern Studies. I've no idea why it's part of an engineering degree, but ...' Lucy raised her eyebrows, 'the lecturer is quite yummy. He's from Palestine, and John is supervising him with a project about getting desalinated water into his country.'

Debra Donaldson looked at her daughter and then turned to her husband. 'This isn't a Palestinian engineer who studied in China and is now promoting a major seawater desalination project in Gaza?'

'Yes ... yes, it is. I'm afraid his application is causing some problems for the university. Perhaps, we should talk about it later.'

'Well, I think he's gorgeous,' said Lucy. And what he's trying to do is very important.' She finished her coffee and bounced from the room with her books.

'I guess you're not driving her to lectures today.'

John Marshall watched his stepdaughter leave and raised his eyebrows. 'I guess not. Anyway, now that she's gone, why did you send Shehadeh to me?'

'What do you mean?' asked Senator Donaldson.

'I've written papers on the desalination of seawater, and I thought his project had merit. But when he approached me to supervise him, he didn't tell me or the university that China was sponsoring the project. That's put me in an embarrassing situation. We would not have accepted his application if we knew all the details.'

'There's something else he didn't tell you?'

'The desalination plant is to be built in Egypt with Chinese money and the water piped across the border into Gaza. So, there's a lot of politics in the background. Americans for Palestine supported his application. Aren't you a member of the group?'

'No. I'm definitely not a member. If I was, the Republicans would crucify me, and I would lose the little Jewish support I have. But I do support what they are trying to do. The Palestinians get a raw deal from Israel.'

'I wish you'd spoken to me about him. My contract with the university is about to be renewed, and this sort of thing may affect it. I know I said it's time I thought of retiring, but I want to leave on my own terms and when I'm good and ready.'

She reached over and gently touched her husband's hand. She sensed tension building between them. It was one of the few times it had happened in their relationship.

'John, I had no idea you would end up being his supervisor. Americans for Palestine asked me to support the application. That's all. My office organises that sort of thing all the time. Your name wasn't mentioned.'

'I wonder why he approached me. His degree from the University of Science and Technology in China would give him the qualifications to build a desalination plant and pipelines.'

'What are you going to do?'

John sighed 'Let it ride. Let's see what the university does. And what do we do about Lucy?'

'Hmm. It looks like she has her eyes on Shehadeh. I'm afraid my daughter is a little out of control at the moment.'

'You know, I'm starting to wonder why he came to America.'

'So am I,' said Senator Debra Donaldson as she returned to staring out the window. 'So am I.'

12

Paul Shehadeh walked along Amsterdam Avenue, leaving Columbia University behind him. He pondered the mission he was undertaking in America. Having Professor Marshall as his supervisor was the first step. The professor was known across the world in the engineering community involved in the desalination of sea water. That he happened to be married to an American senator could be useful. But now the university's Vice Chancellor had banned him speaking about his project to anyone outside the university, he wasn't sure what options were available to him to raise the plight of his people. He was scheduled to speak to Americans for Palestine soon. He needed to get that ban lifted. But how?

'Well, look at you.'

The familiar voice pulled him into the present.

'Hello, Lucy. Hello, Rosa.'

Lucy looked him up and down. 'Dr Shehadeh without a coat and tie, and wearing sunglasses and a Columbia baseball cap. You're settling into university life in America. I'll bet you didn't wear that gear at your Chinese university.'

'Correct, white shirts all the time in China.' He looked at Lucy's blue eyes and smiled. 'I was always scrubbing my collars and trying to wash out stains from the front of my shirts. I took a while to master chopsticks.'

Shehadeh turned to Rosa. 'Now that I know that Lucy is my supervisor's stepdaughter, I will be on my best behaviour with both of you.' He paused. 'I'm going to Down Under to try the new style Australian coffee. Would you like to join me?'

'Thanks, but Lucy and I are off to a game of golf. She thinks she can beat me, but I'm not so sure.'

Lucy smiled at Paul and said to Rosa, 'We've got time for a quick coffee, haven't we? And perhaps Paul can join us for golf next time?'

Paul smiled back at Lucy. 'I'd like that,' he said.

13

Over the following weeks, Shehadeh made it his business to have coffee with Lucy and Rosa. He talked about their assignments, but also about Jacqueline Kennedy Onassis Reservoir, New York City's major water pipelines, Kensico Dam and the valve chamber and filtration plant at Van Cortlandt Park. Occasionally at first, and then more often, he met Lucy without Rosa. He considered it a win when Lucy didn't object. They discussed the lack of water in Palestine, his project and, later, the politics of the Middle East. More and more, she would touch his arm when making a point or when laughing at one of his jokes.

One Saturday, Lucy picked him up in her mother's car. They travelled to Valhalla and parked in the plaza at the foot of Kensico Dam. They walked to The Rising, the memorial commemorating the local men and women killed in the 9/11 attacks, before hiking to the old road that crossed the top of the dam wall. They walked from one side to the other before moving back to the plaza. Paul had brought his camera to take photos of the area, and he noticed a potential shot of Lucy with the dam wall in the background.

'Can I take your photo, Lucy? The light's good.'

'Why not? Like this?'

Lucy lowered her head before flicking her hair back. Paul reversed his baseball cap and took a series of photographs with her hair flowing in the air and another series with her backpack over one shoulder and her face turned towards the camera.

'That's enough,' she said, and she playfully stuck her tongue out at the camera.

'I give you full marks, Jamila,' he said with a smile. 'You look beautiful.'

'Jamila?'

'From now on, Jamila is my private name for you.'

'Where does that come from?'

'From home. Jamila is the name for a beautiful woman.'

The couple walked in silence as they moved towards a mobile lunch van.

'Lunch?' asked Paul.

As they ate, Paul watched Lucy.

'I was talking with Mum about Palestine.'

'Senator Debra Donaldson.'

'How do you know she's a senator?'

'Your mother is very well known in my country. She has tried to improve things.'

'Really?'

'Yes, we appreciate her support.'

'How did you know she was my mother?'

'I knew she was married to your stepfather, but I didn't

work out she was your mother until you came into his office. Why do you ask?'

'She has asked me not to blab about her position. She is constantly concerned that I might be kidnapped or something. I told her she was being silly, but she still worries.'

Lucy finished her burger and wiped mustard from the corner of her mouth.

'Mum has helped me understand what's going on in Palestine.'

Paul nodded, staring into the distance. 'The problems in my country have been happening for a very long time. Since the formation of Israel, more and more Jewish settlers have arrived in my country. Palestinians are now the minority in our own land. Your country has tried to help, but things have not really improved since President Carter brokered a deal between Egypt's President Sadat and Israel's Prime Minister Begin. The takeover of our country continues.'

'What about water? You said the Israelis control the water that goes to Palestine?'

'Everyone knows the Middle East is very dry. Water is important. Your bible and the Quran talk of living water. Living water is a religious concept, but water is the liquid of life. If we are deprived of water, we wither and die. That is what Israel is doing to us. When they fire missiles from their planes, death comes quickly to my people. But they kill us slowly when they don't allow us adequate clean water.'

'Mum says Palestine is getting a raw deal.'

'Yes, we are.' Paul looked into Lucy's eyes. 'Do you think I could have a meeting with your mother to talk about my project?'

'Sure. But will the university allow you to speak to her?

I thought you weren't allowed to speak about it?'

'Who told you that?'

He saw her hesitate. 'Something I heard at home. Anyway, it's time we got out of here. Come on.'

Lucy stood and headed for the exit. As they walked to the parking lot, she took his hand. Paul stopped and held her at arm's length. He looked at her face and the curves of her body, then he closed his eyes and tried to suppress the new tension inside of him.

'Lucy ... no.'

'Come on, you're in America now. The rules are different.'

'I can't. I want your mother's support for my project. Does she know I'm with you today?'

'I said I was with Rosa.'

Paul held Lucy close for a moment and then walked away from her.

'Drop me at my apartment,' he said as he moved towards the car.

'You're no fun,' she said and ran after him.

14

Lucy entered the family's brownstone home in Murray Hill and walked across the highly polished timber floor. Her mother came out from the living room.

'How did it go at Kensico Dam?'

'It was a beautiful day. The sun's quite warm.'

'That's nice. Did you drop Rosa home?'

'Yes, why?'

'Because Rosa called in to say hello.'

Lucy turned quickly. 'Going to the bathroom, Mum.'

Lucy rushed to the bathroom, closed the door and rang Rosa.

'Rosa, it's Lucy. What did you say to Mum?'

'What could I say? You didn't tell me you were going to Kensico Reservoir. You were with Paul, weren't you.'

'You didn't mention his name, did you?'

'Of course not. But you left me in a bind.'

'I didn't know you were going to come over, did I? You should have sent a text.'

Rosa was silent.

'Are you still there?' asked Lucy.

Lucy heard a deep intake of air as Rosa took a breath.

'Are you sure you should be seeing Paul?'

'He's lovely,' said Lucy. 'Look, I've got to go. Mum's calling me for dinner, and I've got to ask her something important.'

'Lucy, be careful.'

'Got to go. Bye.'

At dinner, her mother asked the expected question. 'Who did you take to Kensico Reservoir today?'

There was no escape. She placed her pasta fork on the table. 'Paul Shehadeh.'

Out of the corner of her eye she saw her stepfather stop eating and stare at her.

'Paul would like to meet with you. He would like to speak with you about his project.'

'I'm sorry,' her mother replied, 'but that won't be happening.'

'But why? I thought you supported the Palestinians. Getting clean drinking water to his people is a worthwhile humanitarian cause, surely.'

'He can't be trusted. He lied in his application to Columbia.'

'He didn't lie. He knew if he supplied all the details he wouldn't get into America, let alone Columbia.'

'I supported his application, but he has embarrassed me and your father.'

'You're just being a politician. You're not seeing him because you're up for re-election. That's it, isn't it?'

'Lucy May Donaldson, you are out of line. We'll not discuss this further.'

Lucy softened her voice. 'John, please tell her. You know they need water.'

Her stepfather hesitated.

'Lucy, leave the room,' her mother said.
Lucy threw her napkin on the table and stormed out.

15

He felt the rage simmering: a cauldron of bile burning within him. It was always worse when he remembered the past. His bitterness bubbled higher, attacking his very being. His jaw tightened, but a sharp pain from a cracked tooth stopped him dwelling on the past, and soon the anger subsided.

Leaving his breakfast unfinished, he went to the drawer and took two Tylenol tablets from a packet and swallowed them with his coffee. Slowly, the pain eased, and he found himself thinking about what he had to do. It would be like the old days, and he couldn't wait for his father to find out.

Morning light had not yet emerged in the eastern sky when he walked over to the truck, but light from the streetlamps shone on the paintwork revealing grime and grease from years of transporting garbage. He climbed in the cabin, his clothes as black as the dirt on the truck, and drove along Taconic State Parkway towards Valhalla.

Traffic was light. Nervous excitement moved through his body. He took a left turn off the parkway onto Columbus Avenue and passed the entrance to Kensico Dam Plaza. Two minutes later, he drove past the red bricks of the Methodist United Church, its white steeple barely visible in the light of the quarter moon. A right turn put the truck onto Westlake Drive, with the black waters of Kensico Reservoir running alongside. As he passed North Kensico Avenue, he glanced at his mirrors and then his surroundings. No headlights or house lights lit the darkness. He drove past the sign with ROAD CLOSED written in big bold letters. The other words on the sign were illegible, but he knew what they were. Vehicle entry was prohibited by the Department of Environmental Protection, the department that managed and guarded the water supplies of New York City.

A barrier finally blocked him from driving the truck any further. He pulled over and reached out his gloved hand and turned the ignition key. The clatter of the diesel motor fell silent. He pulled at the edge of his beanie, and it unravelled to become a ski mask that covered his face. Next, he turned off the vehicle's lights and put his right hand underneath the driver's seat. A smile touched his face. His brown eyes looked around the cabin to make sure nothing was left behind. He stepped down from the truck and listened for any movement. There was the distant sound of a vehicle, so he moved quickly to the tree line and stood in the shadows and watched as it travelled slowly along North Kensico Avenue. As it turned into Westlake Drive and drove towards him, he recognised the distinctive outline of a police vehicle. Shit.

As a new graduate, Officer James Lehman of the Department of Environmental Protection Police found himself working security patrols on night shift every three weeks. He just finished his check of Kensico Dam Plaza, the dam holding back the water of Kensico Reservoir, which had supplied water to New York city as far back as 1885 and was now an important storage for water from Upstate.

He was proud to wear the badge of DEP Police. The department had a large budget to maintain New York City's water supply, which meant that its police were well resourced to protect the many reservoirs, water supply dams and wastewater plants scattered across the state. And the department had steadily increased its police numbers and equipment since bin Laden attacked the Twin Towers, which was why there was an opening for him. For the moment he was driving around the streets. But one day he hoped to fly the department's helicopter and had booked to start flying lessons next month.

From Kensico Dam Plaza, he drove his Chevy Tahoe along Columbus Avenue, slowing as he neared the animal hospital. His dog, Pooch, was staying overnight after the removal of a growth. He stopped in the hospital's parking lot, turned off the engine and listened for any crying or barking. His concentration was disturbed as a slow-moving garbage truck turned left from the Parkway onto Columbus. He listened again as the truck moved into the distance, but no noise could be heard from the animal hospital.

'Take care, Pooch. Your dad will see you in a few hours.'

He started to update his electronic log.

Ten minutes later, he fired up his Chevy and drove back to Kensico Avenue to check Westlake Drive, which continued across the top of the new dam wall. Six thousand vehicles crossed the dam wall road prior to 9/11. Now, access was only available to joggers. Occasionally, late at night, he found a young couple making out in their vehicle at the end of the closed road. In most cases, they soon moved off when he shone his headlights on them.

A right turn into Westlake Drive allowed the beam of his headlights to light up the rear reflectors of a vehicle. Flicking to high beam illuminated a large truck. Immediately, his stomach tightened and he called his communication centre.

'Seven zero three, I've got a garbage truck on Westlake Drive at the barrier to the dam. I'll get a plate number to check.'

'Roger 703'.

Officer Lehman moved slowly to within two car lengths to read the number plate, but dirt obscured it.

'Typical,' he muttered, wondering if the driver had pulled in to catch a nap.

He stepped from his vehicle and reached to his holster. He kept his right hand on his gun while using his left hand to shine his torch over the truck, first lighting up the driver's door then quickly checking the rest of the vehicle. Then he slowly moved alongside the truck's rear axle, waiting to see some movement in the cabin.

The small stand of American Sycamore and Sweet Birch trees provided plenty of camouflage. He remained still as he watched the police officer step from his vehicle and walk carefully towards the driver's door of the garbage truck.

Like a panther starting to hunt, he slowly moved from the trees, padding with increasing speed from the shadows. He moved behind the truck and was about an arm's length away when the young officer started to turn. He raised his Glock 26 and fired. The 9 mm bullet smashed into the skull of the police officer.

'You have to do better than that, sucker.'

He quickly looked for the brass cartridge ejected from his pistol but couldn't find it, even with the headlights shining from the police car. He moved to the vehicle and turned off its headlights and motor before standing still and listening. But he could only hear the sound of his own heavy breathing. There were no vehicles, and there was no movement from nearby houses.

He climbed onto the side loader of the garbage truck. Reaching into the top pocket of his coveralls, he removed a small silver cylinder, about half the size of a cigarette, and leaned into the opening where rubbish was dumped. Working quickly, he taped the silver cylinder onto a mobile phone he had pre-set to vibrate in twenty minutes.

Job done, he jumped down from the compactor and again moved to the tree line, where he stopped to look and listen. There were no vehicle lights or house lights showing, but he knew there was a good chance someone could be looking from their house windows. They weren't going to turn on a light to look outside. Satisfied with the stillness, he walked quickly along the tree line running alongside North Kensico Avenue, crossed the Parkway and headed for the parking lot of Valhalla Train Station.

16

Bec walked into the FBI offices. She was back from leave and keen to start working with Musa. She found him at his desk in their open space office. Musa sat at his computer. She knew Jessica had told him they would work together for a trial period and wondered how their first day together would pass. As she reached Musa, she heard footsteps behind her. She turned and was surprised to see her supervisor rushing towards her.

'There's been a truck bombing at Kensico Reservoir,' Jessica White said, breathlessly. 'The boss is sending every free agent to support the investigation. I want you to get over to the Department of Environmental Protection in Queens. They manage the reservoir. Speak to Assistant Commissioner Anderson and offer whatever assistance you can.'

'I guess this is going to be our first job?' she said, as they rushed to the carpool.

'Yep.'

They reached the basement parking lot as the last spare vehicle was driving away.

'Let's take the subway,' said Bec. 'It'll be just as quick this time of day.'

The two agents jumped onto the train at Brooklyn

Bridge–City Hall subway station. Peak hour hadn't finished, and all the seats were still filled with commuters. They moved to the quietest part of the carriage and stood holding onto handrails. Most of the commuters were staring at their phones. A few stared openly at her then pointedly looked at Musa.

At Grand Central, they changed to another train. Eighteen minutes later, they got off at Junction Boulevard, Flushing, and walked along the Boulevard before entering the offices of the Department of Environmental Protection.

Bec walked straight over to Security at the front counter. 'FBI Agents Bekele and Halmat to see Assistant Commissioner Anderson.'

'I won't be a moment.' The woman made a call before turning back to Bec. 'Someone will be down straight away.'

A woman soon emerged from the lift and walked over to them. She wore the uniform of a lieutenant, and the words DEP Police, City of New York were on her cloth arm badges.

'Hi, Terri Heinemann.' she said with a tired, worried look on her face.

'Hi, Bec Bekele, and this is Agent Musa Halmat.'

Terri Heinemann returned a weak smile and walked them to the lift. They got out at level five and entered the office of Patrick O'Shaughnessy, chief of the DEP Police. O'Shaughnessy stood and moved around his desk to greet the two agents. He shook their hands and guided them towards a man rising from his chair.

'This is Assistant Commissioner Paul Anderson. The assistant commissioner leads the Asset Protection and Emergency Response for DEP. I report to the assistant commissioner.

Anderson introduced himself to both agents, and then his eyes briefly returned to Bec before he moved to the business at hand.

'Are there any current threats to DEP assets that we might not know about?' he asked.

'No sir,' Bec replied. 'None that we are aware of. The threat level has not changed since 9/11.'

'Okay, let's get started.' Anderson turned to his chief of police. 'Is the helicopter ready?'

'Yes sir.'

The flight from the DEP building to Kensico Dam took only five minutes in the Leonardo AW119kx. When they were close to the reservoir, Bec spoke through her headset. 'Commissioner, can we do a loop of the reservoir before we land? I'd like to get an overview of the area and see if there are any unauthorised boats.'

'Good idea, but then I need to get down there.'

'Thank you, sir.'

A loop of the reservoir revealed nothing of interest. But before they landed, the pilot flew over the bomb site. They saw the remains of the garbage truck. The crumpled remnants of the cabin were lying on the road on the far side of the barricade. The front wheels and chassis remained where the truck had parked. The top of the rectangular metal compactor was missing, and the sides of the compactor had peeled like a banana skin. The DEP police vehicle was not recognisable.

'Phew,' said Bec involuntarily, half speaking, half expelling air. 'See the metal amongst the trees? That was some explosion.'

'Yeah, it's demolished the front walls of the nearest houses,' said Musa.

'Two bodies were found in the house closest to the explosion,' said the assistant commissioner.

Bec looked at Musa, first one dead police officer and now two civilians killed. The media would run with this story for days, probably longer. The heat would be on law enforcement.

Bec's first thought was the bombing might have been an attempted terrorist attack. Kensico Plaza sits below the dam wall that holds the waters of the reservoir and is a popular recreational area. Throughout the year the plaza hosts events that attract thousands of visitors. But the bombing had taken place in the quiet of the night. If it was a terrorist attack, they failed to maximise the damage.

From the air she could see the local police had stopped all traffic along Westlake Drive, Columbus and Kensico Avenues, as well as the roads contained within them.

'Looks like the crime scene has been properly sealed off,' said Musa.

'Yes, they've done a good job.'

Their DEP pilot headed for a roped area on the lawns next to the parking lots and landed. The FBI helicopter, with personnel from the Evidence Management Unit at Quantico, was already on the ground.

The parking lot was full of assorted police vehicles and trucks. Satellite dishes pointed to the sky. Tents were being erected at the other end of the lawns of the plaza. They were being filled with tables and chairs to service the needs of all the crime scene police, bomb disposal officers from police and military, as well as media officers who were already speaking to fifty or so reporters and their camera crews. The airspace above the reservoir was now closed. But any camera crews that got to the scene early would have managed to get pictures of the bomb site from their helicopters.

Bec led Musa to the forward command tent. Both were now wearing their FBI vests. They went over to a young DEP officer to report their presence. He had to ask them to spell their names several times before he managed to enter them correctly on his computer log.

'Where's the FBI tent?' Bec asked.

The officer, who was now looking very uncomfortable, pointed across the parking lot.

They walked over to the FBI command vehicle. Jessica White was already there, making sure it was functioning efficiently, with agents performing intelligence, media liaison, and communications.

'Just arrived on the DEP helicopter,' said Bec. 'What do you need?'

'You've had a look at the scene from the helicopter?'

'It looks a mess, but it's all sealed off. We did a quick loop around the reservoir but didn't see anything of interest.'

'Okay, see that path over there? Follow it to the top of the dam wall. That's Westlake Drive. That will take you to the bomb site. Make sure everything is under control; and call me once you've made that assessment. Then the two of you can have a look around ... but without stepping on any toes. It's the Department of Environmental Protection's patch. We'll be working together on this. We take charge once it's considered a terrorist bombing. I can't see what else it could be at this stage. So, let's get going. Once it's confirmed that it was a bomb, it's our investigation'.

'Got it,' said Bec, thinking about the many aspects of the investigation to be covered in the days and weeks ahead.

She turned to Musa. 'I'll lead and scan the path. You keep an eye on the surroundings.'

'You're the boss,' replied Musa.

Bec ignored the sarcasm in his voice. She was senior in service, but Musa had more police experience with his ten years in NYPD. She felt that he resented having to report to her.

They moved purposefully along the path, looking for any footprints in soft earth or anything that was unusual. Bec was the first to see the dam wall. It was no Hoover Dam, but it was still impressive in size and appearance. Large granite blocks, elaborately placed, formed the fascia of the wall, making it look like a huge castle rampart protecting some unseen citadel.

When they reached the top of the path, they saw Westlake Drive crossing the dam. The road was lined by more granite blocks. Ornate circles were carved into the stone. They looked like round shields protecting the structure. The finish was a work of art.

'Wow. Impressive,' said Bec.

'Sure is.'

Bec looked back to the plaza, about the length of a football field below. Another marquee was being erected in law enforcement tent city. The two agents crossed the road to look out over the black waters of Kensico Reservoir stretching into the distance.

'Come on. Let's go,' said Bec.

They moved to the bomb site. It was carnage – the truck split open, trees shredded and homes damaged. Officer Lehman's body lay where he fell. He was covered with a groundsheet, but his blood had run from beneath it and congealed on the asphalt.

They were standing at the crime scene tape when Bec's cell phone rang.

'Bekele.'

'Bec, this is Jessica. The explosive guys have found traces of ammonium nitrate. That's not the sort of stuff you carry in a garbage truck, so it is considered a terrorist incident. You and Musa are to take charge of the crime scene. Everything now goes through FBI command.'

17

Bec and Musa were seated in the second row of the conference room in the FBI offices in New York. Alongside them were Jessica White, the crime scene commander and other FBI specialists from their laboratories at Quantico and Alabama. Behind them, more specialists from the different agencies sat waiting for the top brass to arrive so the meeting could begin. Those who knew each other chatted quietly.

The Commissioner of the Department of Environmental Protection arrived with a frown and dark bags under his eyes. Robert Blum, the special agent in charge of the New York office, was waiting just inside the conference room door and directed him to a front row seat. Senior representatives from the governor's and mayor's offices arrived together, followed by the deputy Commissioner of New York's city police and the chief of the DEP Police.

Once everyone was seated, Blum called on the DEP's commissioner to address the group. The commissioner gave an overview of his department.

'Most of you know that the Department of Environmental Protection reports to the Mayor of New York, but we operate across the whole state. We manage and protect our nineteen reservoirs, twenty-nine water supply dams and seven wastewater plants, and we employ 3,000 people. Sadly, one of our employees, Officer James Lehman, was murdered while on patrol keeping New York's water infrastructure safe. And that's why we are here today. It is our duty to find the perpetrator of this heinous crime and remove the risk to our water supplies.'

The commissioner handed over to his chief engineer, who was seated at the rear of the room. He spoke about how Kensico Reservoir had supplied water to New York City as far back as 1885 and was now an important storage reservoir for water from Upstate before being piped to the city.

'If an explosion was designed to breach the dam wall, Valhalla to the Bronx would be hit by a wall of water.'

The representatives from the governor's and the mayor's offices glanced at one another before the governor's rep spoke. 'How many people would be impacted if the dam wall was breached?'

'Two hundred thousand people live downstream from the dam wall. The number of lives lost would depend on the time of day. Modelling suggests that more people would be affected during the day when people are driving around. Roads would become flooded, and people would be trapped in their cars. Blocked roads prevent the quick rescue of trapped people. We feel people would get some protection at night if they were in their homes, provided those homes were not completely destroyed by the impact of the water.'

The DEP commissioner interrupted.

'The primary impact of a breach of the dam wall is flooding. The secondary impact is the loss of water to New York City. Ninety per cent of the city's water flows through

Kensico Reservoir. Nine million people would be without water.' Beads of sweat broke out on his forehead as he continued. 'Nine million.'

There was silence in the room as the commissioner's words hit home. It was Bec's boss, Agent Blum, who broke the silence.

'Thank you, commissioner. Let's not forget that three people have already died in the bombing. As the commissioner said, Officer Lehman was shot just before the explosion. And the blast killed Giuseppe and Sylvia Romeo. Sylvia Romeo called the Mt Pleasant police communication centre at 0448 hours. She reported a shot that woke her from her sleep. Mrs Romeo told the operator she saw car lights being turned off on the section of old Westlake Drive that continues over the dam wall and was going to go back to bed but saw someone in dark clothing moving quickly along Kensico Avenue towards Columbus. You know the rest. Twenty-three homes were damaged by the blast.'

Robert Blum quickly moved on.

'Agent White supervised the crime scene once it was declared a terrorist act. I'll ask her to say a few words.'

Jessica White rose from her chair. As she moved to the front of the room, she pushed a button on the remote in her hand and a screen lowered from the ceiling. Another push of a button switched on the data projector. Bec had seen most of the photographs previously, but Jessica had added arrows highlighting important points in the photos. Questions were answered and features in the photographs were highlighted with the remote which doubled as a laser pointer.

The picture of a garbage truck filled the screen.

'The explosive was carried in a White-GMC with a Heil Rapid Rail automated side loader. They are very common, and second-hand garbage trucks can be bought on internet sites such as TruckHelp.'

She paused for a moment.

'But the truck driven by the bomber was stolen from a recycling depot in West Milford two weeks ago. The depot also does private garbage collection on an ad hoc basis. The lock on the gate was cut. Most likely industrial bolt cutters were used. The office door was jemmied to get the keys and the truck driven away. The depot was not alarmed, so the theft was not reported until the next morning. We are checking CCTV in the district for vehicles approaching the depot and the truck being driven away. Nothing yet.'

A red dot from the laser pointer hit the screen.

'The side loader truck is what you typically see in the suburbs. A hydraulic arm lifts garbage bins and tips the rubbish into the hopper behind the cabin. Then, the rubbish is pushed by a hydraulically operated packing plate into the bin at the back of the truck. The packing plate seals the rubbish bin. A small explosion would be contained within the bin, but this one had sufficient force to blow it apart, sending metal in all directions.'

The room remained quiet. Jessica continued.

'We believe ammonium nitrate was used for the explosion. We're still determining the amount used, and we haven't found traces of a detonator yet. Small fragments of a cell phone were found. Most likely, it was a timed detonation, but this still needs to be confirmed.'

Bec listened carefully as her supervisor continued. The strength of her old partner's talk impressed her.

'Ammonium nitrate is used all over the world as a fertilizer and an explosive. Three tons of it was used for the 1995 Oklahoma City bombing. More recently, the explosion in Beirut was ammonium nitrate fertilizer. Two thousand tons of it was poorly stored in a Beirut warehouse for six years. The Beirut explosion was one of the biggest non-nuclear explosions in history.'

A picture of Officer Lehman's body at the scene was next. His police chief looked down and closed his eyes.

'Officer Lehman was shot in the head. His body was largely intact because the blast exploded upwards and outwards passing over his body. Crime Scene looked for the remains of a suicide bomber; someone who triggered the blast while in the truck. As you know, explosives will rip a body apart, but a person's head or limbs are often found. No body parts were discovered.' Jessica paused again. 'So, we believe it was a timed explosion or triggered remotely.'

The flattened Chevy police vehicle and the White-GMC garbage truck were shown from different angles.

'The blast blew apart the metal sides of the compactor of the garbage truck, causing a fireball to rise into the air. The fireball was seen for miles. The blast radiated outwards smashing into Officer Lehman's car, breaking its windshield and flattening its roof.'

Another picture.

'Nearby trees were stripped of their leaves before the shock wave reached homes on Westlake Drive. The three closest homes had one or more of their exterior walls demolished, and twenty other homes were damaged.'

Photographs of Sylvia and Giuseppe Romeo.

'Glass shredded Sylvia Romeo's face and upper body, so

we believe she was still looking from her bedroom window when the shock wave hit her. Giuseppe Romeo died in his bed. The next day, Crime Scene found the casing of the nine-millimetre slug that killed Officer Lehman. It was a nine-millimetre Parabellum round. We know that round is used in many pistols. So, not much help there. But investigators spent ten hours using a metal detector with different settings to sweep the bomb site once the patrol vehicle and larger truck pieces were removed. They found the casing of a nine-millimetre metal jacket bullet in the tree line, close to where Lehman's body fell. That will help ballistics match it with a gun when we get a suspect.'

Bec appreciated the 'when we get a suspect' not 'if'. They would get whoever was behind this.

At the end of the meeting, different groups mingled talking in hushed tones. Bec saw the tall DEP assistant commissioner moving towards them, a slight smile on his face. He was a little overweight but had the poise of someone who had power and used that power to control people.

'Agents Bekele and Halmat, good to see you again.' He briefly looked at Musa before concentrating on Bec. 'If you want any assistance in any way, please do not hesitate to ask.'

'Thank you, Commissioner.' Bec saw the way the assistant commissioner looked at her and she guessed what might happen next.

'Bec, you remind me of a model. Perhaps someone in your family?'

Bec glanced at Musa standing slightly behind the assistant commissioner. Musa had the faintest grin on his normally deadpan face. She knew Musa had seen a similar approach when they were at Quantico. With someone like the assistant commissioner, Musa does not exist. But she knew he didn't mind. They were already talking about how to use such situations to their advantage. Bec would charm the bad guys, and Musa would take them down if the charm offensive didn't work.

'My sister has done a bit of modelling, but I stick to basketball.'

Bec returned a professional smile – friendly and polite. She had another one for special occasions.

18

Bec scanned the preliminary lab report on the bombing. The file consisted of fifty pages of technical information. She understood a lot of the details because of her experience while working with Jessica on the parcel post bomber. She wondered how Musa would go with it. Time would tell. She blanked her screen and looked over at Musa, who was concentrating on his own files.

'Come on. Let's get out of here,' she said.

'Just a minute.'

He continued looking at his screen. A photograph appeared to have grabbed his attention. He kept returning to it as he waded through the folder. After a few minutes, he turned to Bec. 'Need a break?'

Bec expelled some air and raised her eyebrows. 'I need to get away from all the files. We're not going to solve this by staring at a computer screen.'

'I was hoping you'd say something like that.'

Bec knew that crimes like this were either solved by luck, by someone nominating a likely suspect or by sheer hard work, where bits of a jigsaw are slowly pieced together. If Officer Lehman was more experienced or a little luckier, he may have apprehended the bomber and been alive to receive a medal. The usual crank callers nominated a few groups and individuals as suspects to the FBI's 'Submit a Tip'. All tips were investigated, but none were nominating anyone of serious interest. Bec felt the investigation was unlikely to progress unless an agent talked to someone who knew something. This investigation was going to be a long, hard grind.

Every spare agent in New York's FBI office was involved in the investigation. One agent from the intelligence unit was chasing the history of the truck used for the bombing and the recycling depot from where it was taken. Another four agents in the unit were researching manufacturers and distributors of ammonium nitrate, the chemical used in the explosion. And Crime Scene was trying to find evidence about the cell phone that was used to initiate the blast, but they weren't having much success finding a serial number. Jessica White coordinated everything in the office, ensuring that statements were being collected and filed on the office's computers. The last two agents from intelligence had started flow charts, which were used to link different people and activities. Another four agents from the office scoured the district around Kensico Dam trying to find CCTV of the truck.

'Let's drive over to West Milford. I want to see the recycling depot where the truck was stolen,' Bec said, heading for the door.

An hour later, they drove into the yard of the run-down recycling depot and parked in front of the portable office building. An old black American came out and watched as they got out of their car.

As Bec approached him, he tried to stretch the arch from his back.

'Well, look at you,' he said. 'You're blacker'n me and twice as tall.'

He turned his attention to Musa. 'Where you from, young fella?'

'New York.'

The old man giggled. 'Middle East, I reckon. If you're reporters, I got nothing more to say.'

'I'm Agent Bekele and this is Agent Halmat. We're from the FBI office in New York.'

'Halmat, eh. I was right about the Middle East then.'

'My father was from Iraq, but he was Kurdish.'

Bec did not bother to mention that her parents were born in Ethiopia,

The old man chuckled again. 'I didn't know the FBI was so multicultural. How can I help you folk? I've already given a statement.'

'We've read your statement,' said Bec, smiling. 'Would you mind showing us around? We'd like to see where you kept the truck keys and where the truck was parked.'

The old man gave a slight bow. 'Young lady, it would be my pleasure. Come in.'

He took them into the office and showed them a rectangular box on the wall. When he opened the box, it contained two sets of vehicle keys and one set of office keys.

'They cut the chain on the front gate, jemmied the front door and took the keys to the truck. But you would know that anyway.'

'Yes, we saw that in your statement,' said Bec. 'Could you show us where the truck was parked?'

He took them to the rear of the building. His old Chevy truck was parked under a carport next to a White-GMC garbage truck. It was a front loader.

'Was this garbage truck in the yard when the other one was stolen?' asked Musa.

A light plane flew low overhead as it approached Greenwood Lake Airport. The old man looked up at the plane. 'Noisy things. They're flying all day.'

Musa repeated his question. 'This truck was in the yard next to the stolen one?'

'Yes, it was. They were parked alongside each other. But no-one's going to get this one. I've installed an alarm system in the office.'

'And the keys for this truck were in the box in the office as well?' Musa asked.

'Yes, they were.'

'Thank you, sir. I'm sure the alarm will do the trick for you.'

'I hope so. I don't have insurance. It's expensive.'

Musa nodded to the old man. 'Okay, you take care now.'

'I sure will.'

19

'I'll drive,' said Musa, as they walked towards their vehicle.

'About time.' She smiled, knowing he always wanted to drive. She put it down to a male ego thing. 'What are you thinking?'

'I want to have another look at the bomb site at Kensico Dam.'

'What for?'

'Tell you later.'

'No, tell me now. I want to know.'

'It's a surprise.'

Musa drove their car from the yard to Valhalla. He passed the entrance to Kensico Dam Plaza and stopped at the crime scene tape on Westlake Drive. The police guard had ended two days before when Crime Scene finished their work, but the tape was left in case they needed to return. They walked to the barricade that crossed Westlake Drive. Musa examined the concrete blocks which were scarred by the explosion and nodded his head several times before turning to Bec.

'What do you see?'

Bec looked around. 'Nothing. Same as before. Obviously, all the mess has gone.'

'What sort of truck carried the explosive?'

'A White-GMC with a Heil Rapid Rail automated side loader,' she said without hesitation.

'And what did we see at the yard?'

'Another White-GMC. It was probably a bit older, and it was a front loader.'

'And?' said Musa. 'You're the senior agent. You should have spotted it by now.'

Bec look at him and her eyes narrowed. He was watching her. She knew that he had seen something. He was looking at crime scene photographs in the office before they left. And his questioning of old Joe at the recycling depot was interesting. He was using his police experience from NYPD, but she was not going to give up quickly. Unhurriedly, she walked to the mark on the road where the asphalt had melted from the explosion and looked around. Slowly, deliberately, she turned three hundred and sixty degrees, looking at the trees stripped of their leaves and the damaged houses behind them and then back to Musa, who was sitting on the barricade one car length away watching her. She crossed her arms and stared past him into the distance, her body automatically falling into its thoughtful pose, with her hips pushed forward and pouting like her sister on the catwalk. A full minute passed as she stood, not moving. Her eyes returned to Musa. She looked at him, and a broad grin spread across her face.

'The barricade,' she called out. 'There's no indication the barricade was breached. The other truck, the front loader, could have moved the barricade. The side loader had nothing at the front to move or push through it.'

Musa kept a straight face. 'You know, Semra Bekele, one day you will be a good agent.'

Bec gave him a one finger salute.

Bec joined Musa at the barricade, and they examined it closely. Flying metal from the explosion had left pock marks on many sections, but they couldn't see any attempt to push through it.

They stood at the barricade a while longer, both reflecting on the significance of their discovery.

'They didn't want to breach the dam,' said Bec. 'If they wanted to, they would have taken the front loader. The prongs on the front could have moved parts of the barricade.'

'Either that or they weren't very smart,' said Musa. 'Why not steal the front loader and fill it with explosives? The front loader could push through the stone road wall on top of the dam, and then they could have driven the truck off the road and into the water for the explosion. Boom! One big flood and no water for New York City.'

Bec nodded. 'They were smart enough to make a truck bomb but not smart enough to get to the top of the dam wall.' She thought for a while before saying, 'Okay, let's get back to the office and tell Jessica what we're thinking.

She walked towards their vehicle. Ex-New York cop Musa Halmat could be grumpy at times, but he could teach her a few things.

20

Senator Debra Donaldson entered the offices of the Senate majority leader.

'Hello, Jean, the Senator asked me to come over. He said it was important.'

The large suite of rooms was twice the size of her rooms on the second floor of Hart Senate Office Building in Washington. When she entered the senator's large office, with its sixteen-foot-high ceilings, three men were there, two of them seated.

Democratic Senator Robert J Birmingham stood and came over to greet her. 'Debra, thanks for coming so promptly. I hope I didn't drag you out of a meeting.'

'The Foreign Affairs Committee finished half an hour ago. I came straight away. You said it was important.'

'You know Director Hill from the Central Intelligence Agency. He's here to brief me on a matter and asked if you could come over. It seems the Chinese are planning to build a base in the Sinai as a part of their Belt and Road Initiative.'

Debra Donaldson immediately thought of her husband and his new research fellow, Shehadeh. She felt acid rising from her stomach but tried to remain relaxed. 'Is it okay if I sit down?'

'Of course. Can I get you some water?'

Birmingham placed a glass of water on the small table alongside her chair. She desperately wanted to drink from it but was afraid her hand would shake if she lifted the glass.

'Director Hill will explain what this is all about.'

'It seems the Chinese are planning a base at Arish in the Sinai. A base there, at the Mediterranean end of the Suez Canal, will complement their existing base in Djibouti on the southern end. This allows them to protect their shipping. Of course, if things become more difficult in the world, the Chinese would be in a position to block the vessels of other countries entering the canal.'

'This is a very worrying development,' added the Senate leader.

'The Egyptians are prepared to go along with it,' the director continued, 'if the Chinese can supply a suitable reason to the world community for placing it there. The Chinese suggested a desalination plant at Arish, to supply piped water to Gaza. A nice humanitarian touch, don't you think?'

'Yes, a clever move,' said Debra. 'Coincidently, there was a briefing paper about it presented to the Foreign Affairs Committee this morning.'

'So, you know all about it?'

Debra lifted her glass and managed to keep her hand from shaking as she sipped some water. This meeting wasn't a coincidence at all. 'Yes, the Chinese were considering a request from the Palestinians to build a large desalination plant in Gaza. This proposal provides a reason for their base at Arish.'

'What? Are they serious?' asked the Senate majority leader.

The CIA Director looked at her before answering. 'Yes, they are.'

'Christ, does the President know?

'I briefed him yesterday,' said the director.

'The committee briefing paper mentioned that the Palestinian engineer working with the Chinese wants to extend the pipeline into the West Bank,' said Debra.

'From the Sinai into Gaza and the West Bank?' The Senate majority leader looked aghast.

'Yes,' replied Debra.

'Well, that would change the dynamics between Israel and Palestine. Is that why you're here Robert?'

'Yes, the pipeline certainly would change the dynamics between Israel and Palestine. But there's another reason why I'm——'

Senator Debra Donaldson interrupted. 'The director may be here to tell you my husband is supervising the Palestinian engineer who is working with the Chinese on the project.'

'I see,' said the Senate majority leader. 'Why is this engineer in America?'

'He's researching desalination technology,' said the director. 'But our sources in the Middle East believe he wishes to gain support for the water pipeline from influential Americans. We believe he is trying to reach Senator Donaldson through her husband, who is supervising him.'

The Senate majority leader responded quickly. 'There's no point in getting support from us. The Chinese are sponsoring the project. They're not going to let us get involved. What's his real reason for coming to America?'

'We're not sure.'

'You're not sure?'

'We're treating him as a potential security risk. And we need to assess this latest Chinese move for a base in the Sinai.'

Debra placed her glass of water on the table. She knew that, at the very least, electronic surveillance would be placed on Shehadeh, and that would bring Lucy to the attention of the CIA.

21

Paul Shehadeh arrived early and stood at the west gate to Columbia University waiting for Lucy and Rosa to arrive. The sun was out, and traffic had eased, bringing a feeling of calmness to the morning. Lucy had talked about them having a game of golf, and Paul had suggested the golf course at Van Cortlandt Park. He saw Lucy approaching from the university grounds and took the opportunity to admire her.

'Where's Rosa?' he asked when she reached him.

'She rang last night to say she couldn't make it, something about having an assignment. There's a train in ten minutes. Shall we catch it?'

Paul nodded. They moved to the subway entrance on the corner of 116th Street and Broadway and jumped on the Line 1 train for the fifty-minute journey to Van Cortlandt Park. After five minutes, Paul spoke. 'Have you asked your mother if I can speak with her about my project?'

'She's thinking about it, so I'm going to work on my stepfather to see if he can convince her to see you.'

As the train rocked and rattled to their destination, both checked and read messages on their iPhones.

Paul stood and stretched to leave the train at Van

Cortlandt Park station. 'Okay, are you ready to be beaten at golf?'

'No way. I can hold my own,' Lucy said, grabbing her backpack from between her legs. 'What's your handicap?'

'I don't have a handicap.'

Lucy gave him a playful shove. 'Well ... look out then.'

They headed for the Mosholu Golf Club, fifteen minutes away. Paul stopped twice on the way and looked around.

'Green, so much green. That's not something you see in Palestine.'

They played the nine-hole course in two hours. Paul's tee shots were thirty yards further along the course, and most landed on the fairway. But Lucy's short game was superior, and she won every hole but one. At the end of the game, Paul leaned over and kissed her on the cheek.

'Well done. You were too good.'

Lucy's face flushed. 'Your short game let you down. You spent too much time on the driving range in China.'

'You're right. Everyone in China wants to drive the ball over the horizon.'

'You had me on the fifth, but the sun got in your eyes. What happened to your baseball cap?'

'I think someone must have picked it up at the barber's thinking it was theirs. I've been meaning to go to the university shop to get another one.'

'There's a pitching range near here. Why don't we find it and have some practice shots? Your pitching needs some work.'

'Great. You remember I talked about a valve chamber directing water to New York.'

'It rings a bell. What's special about it?'

'The valve chamber is two hundred and fifty feet below the pitching range. It's huge. People don't realise. The vaulted ceiling is as high as a three-story building. Your stepfather tried to get me permission to see it, but permission was refused.'

'Why wouldn't you be allowed to see it?'

'No visitors are allowed anymore. They're worried about terrorism. That's why it is buried underground.'

Paul and Lucy moved behind the club rooms to a wall surrounding a large circular practice area about twice the size of a football field. There were several signs saying, 'area closed'.

'It's huge,' said Lucy. 'I've never seen anything like it.'

'Underneath is the valve chamber and a water filtration plant. Water flowing to New York City is managed here. The valve chamber is the junction for all the pipes that supply water to the Bronx, Manhattan, Queens and Brooklyn.'

Paul took Lucy's hand and placed it on his chest.

'Think of my heart as a valve chamber that has arteries bringing and sending blood to my body. Underneath us is New York's heart. It cost billions of dollars. It makes my project look small.'

Lucy smiled as he held her hand.

'Can you imagine if something happened here?' said Shehadeh.

The glow in Lucy's face quickly vanished, and she removed her hand. 'What do you mean?'

'If this valve chamber stopped working, all of New York City would be without water. Americans would know what it is like to be without water.'

'That's a terrible thing to say.'

'Why?' said Paul. 'It's true.'

'Don't even think about something going wrong in New York. Not after 9/11. We've suffered so much.'

'And we lost the same number of people when Israel invaded Gaza in 2014.'

Paul reached out and held her hands. 'Please ... water is everything to us. My people have so little water. It is so important that Americans realise what my people are going through. Americans are the only ones who can help us.'

Lucy wiped away his tears with her fingers and took him into her arms. He stared over her shoulder looking at the rolling green turf of the practice area.

22

'What have we got?' asked Bec, as she and Musa entered Jessica White's office in the FBI building in New York.

'Come in. Shut the door.'

They sat opposite their supervising agent and waited while she methodically worked a pile of photographs into order. Bec glimpsed a photograph of Kensico Dam wall amongst them.

'The people at Submit a Tip have received calls nominating various groups responsible for the bombing,' said Jessica, opening the file on her desk. 'Al-Qaeda has been mentioned about fifty times, but the CIA has heard no chatter about their possible involvement.'

'I thought they're restricted to Syria and north-western Iraq now,' said Bec.

'True, and mostly through links with ISIS, but we can't rule them out yet because of their association with other groups.'

'What about Al-Shabaab?' asked Musa.

'We've had another five groups nominated as possible suspects. Al-Shabaab was one of them. The remaining four are right wing groups based here in America. Intelligence and our offices near where those groups are located are looking into these leads.'

Jessica looked at another page in the file. 'Another forty-nine individuals have been nominated: all Americans or residents living in the States. We're making the normal enquiries on those leads.' She paused and looked at Bec. 'One has stood out. I want you to take the lead on this one. An anonymous caller suggested we should have a look at a Nasir Shehadeh. He's a Palestinian engineer studying and teaching at Columbia here in New York. Here's his passport photograph.'

Bec took the photograph and stared at the face of Shehadeh before pushing it towards Musa. He grabbed it from the desk.

'What makes him special?' he asked, abruptly.

Jessica's jaw tightened for a second. 'He wasn't. Not until we saw these.' She passed over twenty photographs of Kensico Plaza. 'Intelligence has been going through all the CCTV footage at Kensico Dam. They started at the time of the bombing and went back one month. Facial recognition compared people visiting the reservoir with images of nominated suspects. Shehadeh came up as a match.'

While Jessica talked, Bec thumbed through the photographs.

'There,' she said.

Musa looked at Bec. 'What?'

'The couple in the photos. The guy is Shehadeh. You can see his face when he turns his baseball cap around to take some photographs.'

Bec and Musa slowly worked through the pictures. They found Shehadeh walking with a young woman across

the plaza. Other pictures showed Shehadeh photographing the dam wall with the woman standing nearby. They
looked like tourists. He was photographing the area while
she stood nearby carrying a backpack.

'Okay,' said Musa, his demeanour softer now.
'Interesting. When were the pictures taken?'

'Two weeks before the explosion.'

'Do we know who the woman is?' asked Bec.

'No, that's what you're going to find out.'

23

Within twelve hours, Bec had organised surveillance on Shehadeh. The early surveillance logs, which were being collated by intelligence, showed her he spent most of his time in the vicinity of Columbia University. She learned that Shehadeh had been using Paul as his first name since he arrived in America.

'You know, I think we have a bum Middle Eastern lead,' said Musa, when he entered their office space.

'Oh, come on. We just started looking at him.'

'No, you think about it.'

For the first time, Bec saw Musa become animated.

'Okay, he's Palestinian; that can fit. We've learnt he's concerned about a lack of water in his country. That also can fit with a bombing at a dam. But we still have no Palestinian or Islamic group claiming responsibility for the bombing. He can't raise the profile of water problems in his country if a political group makes no claim to the bombing or give no reason for doing it.'

'The bombing only happened a week ago,' said Bec, shaking her head.

Jessica White pushed open the door and hurried towards them. 'We think we know where they got the ammonium nitrate. State Parks has a quarry in Sterling Forest. The explosive store was broken into, and 120 bags of ANFO were stolen.'

'ANFO? What's ANFO?' asked Bec.

'I had to ask, as well. It's a mix of ammonium nitrate and six percent diesel. ANFO is a brand name. It comes in plastic bags containing prills, small round balls, like the type of stuff you put on your garden as fertilizer. ANFO prills are pink.'

'When was it reported missing?' Bec asked.

'This morning.'

'It wasn't reported earlier?'

'Parks took over a private quarry a number of years ago. They only extract stone when it is needed for a government job. Yesterday, the manager from the Office of Parks was contacted by one of our teams. They went and checked the explosive store and found the theft.'

'Wasn't the store alarmed?' asked Musa.

'The alarm hasn't been working for three months. It was supposed to be fixed, but it seems no-one got around to it.'

'Good one,' said Musa, quietly.

Bec was thinking. 'The lab people from Huntsville, Alabama, have finished their analysis of the explosive. Can you get them to fly in and give a presentation to the teams who are looking at chemical outlets? We need to give them as much information as possible about the explosives.'

'Good idea,' said Jessica. 'I'll speak to the boss about it.'

24

There were about a hundred FBI personnel crammed into the theatre – agents, crime scene and ballistic specialists and just about every boss working in the New York office – for the presentation by experts from the Terrorist Explosive Device Analytical Centre that Jessica had managed to arrange. Despite the presentation being Bec's suggestion, she'd failed to score a front row seat and was sitting with Musa in the third row, just behind Jessica White.

Robert Blum introduced Special Agent Joseph Fredricks and he said a few words about the analytical centre.

'TEDAC is a multi-agency organisation that gathers intelligence by analysing explosive devices from around the world. It helps our fight against terrorism, and I can tell you that our director is watching this investigation very closely. When you think about it, nothing is more important to our cities than continuous clean water.'

Fredricks introduced his scientific expert, Doctor Jodie Underwood, explaining that she helped with the investigations of the Boston Marathon and Oklahoma City bombings and regularly gave presentations around the world on her findings.

'Let's start with ammonium nitrate,' she said, as pictures of the chemical appeared on the screen. 'It is widely used around the world. In the US, we produce about one million tons per year. Across the world, half of the production is used as explosives and the other half as a fertilizer.'

The group listened in silence.

'Explosive-grade ammonium nitrate has been regulated at the federal level since 1971 and is relatively easy to trace. The sale of ammonium nitrate fertilizer, however, is not regulated in most states. We know that 120 bags of ANFO were stolen from a State Park quarry, and that is the most likely source of the ammonium nitrate. One bag weighs twenty-five kilograms, so three tons of explosive were stolen. The bags are transported on pallets. Each pallet, when loaded with explosive, weighs one ton. Obviously, a truck is needed to move that amount.'

Bec raised her hand. 'How much explosive force from a hundred and twenty bags?'

'You're one step ahead of me. Forty bags of ANFO amount to one ton of explosive. Four tons of explosives were used in the Oklahoma City bombing. We believe sixty bags were used in the Kensico Dam explosion. If the source of the ammonium nitrate was from the quarry, there are another sixty bags out there.'

A buzz started around the room at the possibility of another explosion, and the doctor had to pause to allow the chatter to stop.

'We've found that another chemical was used as well as ammonium nitrate. That chemical is dichloroacetylene. TEDAC is a multi-agency grouping from FBI, Department of Alcohol, Tobacco, Firearms and Explosives, and the

Department of Defense. We have partner agencies across the world. No-one is aware of dichloroacetylene being used previously in a bombing. It was first produced in the early twentieth century. It's highly explosive but dangerous to handle. It is an oil at ordinary temperatures and a colourless gas at elevated temperatures.'

'What about the military?' asked Musa.

'No, it's too volatile. It's also toxic.'

'Does anyone produce it?'

'It's not produced commercially, for the same reasons the military don't use it. So, we're working on the assumption that the bomber made it to cause a larger explosion.'

'How would it be made?' asked Bec.

'Most likely by mixing lye with cleaning fluid. Lye is the common name for caustic soda or sodium hydroxide. Dichloroacetylene is formed when you mix it with trichloroacetylene, our good old cleaning fluid. Both caustic soda and trichloroacetylene can be obtained anywhere. Small amounts of caustic soda are sold in plastic containers of white crystals while larger amounts are usually sold as a liquid, again in plastic containers.'

'What's caustic soda used for?' asked Agent Graham Jacobs from the back of the room.

'Many, many things. The main uses are for the manufacture of pulp and paper, alumina, soap and detergents, petroleum products and chemical production. It is also used for water treatment, food and textiles production, metal processing, mining and glass making. America makes fourteen million tons of caustic soda a year.'

That doesn't help us,' Bec quietly said to Musa. 'We'll be checking those industries for years.'

'Dichloroacetylene will explode if it is exposed to shock, heat, friction or even air. It needs to be stored in cool, well-ventilated areas. We're thinking that the heat and flames from exploding ammonium nitrate set off the dichloroacetylene and added to the explosion. So, look for an indoor storage area and possibly a coolroom to keep it stable. Separately, ammonium nitrate, caustic soda and cleaning fluid are stable. If you think that you have found dichloroacetylene, back off and call your explosives experts.'

'Oh yeh,' said Jacobs, who was close to retirement. 'No problems about that.'

25

As the investigation continued, Bec had noticed that Musa had become even quieter since announcing that Shehadeh was an unlikely suspect.

'You alright?' she asked.

'Yeah, except no-one's listening.'

'What do you mean?'

'There's not much to indicate Shehadeh did the bombing. Someone's nominated him, and he was at the reservoir. What else have we got?'

'He has a motive and we've discovered he wants to raise the profile of water shortages in Palestine. But I'm not arguing with you. We've got a job to do.'

It was time to get out of the office. Bec wasn't staying there checking surveillance logs any longer. 'Do you know Port Jervis? There's a chemical warehouse I want to check out.'

'Why that one? There's a few on the list.'

'It's reasonably close to the depot where the truck was stolen, that's all. It's worth a look. You know how to get there?'

'I know how to get there.' Musa tossed the car remote to her. 'About half an hour northwest of here. Get onto Route 23.'

'So, I'm driving? I thought you always wanted to drive.'

'I'm tired of driving, Miss Daisy. Besides, it's time you learned your way around.'

'Ouch.'

Bec wasn't going to get into an argument over that one. Getting out of the office and talking to people might help clear the air.

Forty-five minutes later, they drove into the industrial estate on the outskirts of Port Jervis. The universal precast concrete warehouse with an office at the front sat amongst six others. Three vehicles were parked out front: a white Lexus LS sedan, an expensive black BMW sedan and an older black BMW SUV.

Musa whistled. 'Look at the Lexus: top of the range. The chemical business must be booming.'

Bec groaned at the pun. 'That's terrible.'

She parked alongside the BMW, and they walked over to the front door. Two young men were behind the counter. One was dressed in slacks and an open neck shirt while the other was dressed in high vis clothing.

'Hello,' said the one in slacks, after staring at them for a few moments. 'Can I help you?'

Bec smiled. 'Hi, I'm Agent Bekele and this is Agent Halmat from the FBI. Can I speak to the manager please?'

He turned to the other young man. 'We'll talk later.'

Bec watched the guy in high vis as he walked out back towards the warehouse.

'He's in a meeting. I'm his son. Perhaps I can help you.'

'We're making enquiries about the bombing at Kensico Dam. We're speaking with chemical suppliers in the district.'

'Just a moment.'

The young man left the reception area and moved to a nearby door. As it opened, Bec could see a corridor with doors on either side, but the door from the reception area closed before she could see how far the young man travelled to speak to his father. He returned after a few minutes, and Bec stopped looking at the paperwork on the reception counter.

'He won't be long. He's just finishing a call.'

'Thank you.'

Bec hadn't seen any lights showing on the digital desk phone, so presumably the manager was on his cell phone.

The manager came to the reception area after a couple of minutes. 'Hi. John Tomlin. How can I help?'

Bec smiled at Tomlin and repeated her introduction.

'Are you the owner?'

'No, just the manager. Industrial Chemical Supplies is owned by a group in Delaware.'

'We're making enquiries about the bombing at Kensico Dam and speaking with chemical suppliers in the district.'

'Yeah, I expected we'd get a visit.'

Bec's cell rang. The screen showed it was a call from the office.

'Excuse me.'

She stepped outside the building and the sun hit her eyes. But she was able to see the white Lexus sedan driving quietly from the yard.

'Hello.'

'Bec, it's Jessica. Come back to the office, we've got a meeting with the boss.'

Bec returned inside. 'Sorry, we've got to go. We'll contact you again later.'

'Sure,' said Tomlin and Bec moved to leave.

She saw that Musa was not following her. He stood looking at John Tomlin. 'Mr Tomlin, did you serve in the Middle East?'

A surprised look came over Tomlin's face. 'Yes, why?'

'I've been given a file about missing artefacts from Iraq. Your name was mentioned as someone who may be able to shed some light on our enquiries.'

Tomlin took a moment to find his words. 'That was a long time ago.'

'Musa, we need to go.'

'If you don't mind, Mr Tomlin,' said Musa, 'we can talk another time.'

'Sure.'

Musa drove from the yard. 'Did you see that look Tomlin gave me when I asked about the missing artefacts?'

'Sure did. That was one guilty look. He knows something about them. But that's for another time.'

26

John Tomlin stood at the front door of his office and watched the two FBI agents drive from the yard. He remained standing looking into the distance long after their car disappeared from his sight, before turning slowly and stepping inside. He looked at his son, who was seated in front of the office computer, then returned to his room and slammed the door.

Tomlin stood in the centre of his office. His heart was beating faster than normal. His breathing was stressed and forced. He returned to his desk to continue his work but found it impossible. He looked out of his window at a tree in the distance that always reminded him of a similar one in the grounds of the hotel in Baghdad where he stayed years ago.

A gust of wind rattled the window of his office and snapped him from his memories. His heartbeat slowed and his breathing had settled. He moved to a small storeroom attached to his office. At the rear of it, a safe had been bolted to the concrete floor. John Tomlin punched his son's birthdate into the electronic touch buttons and the door popped open. He reached to the back and removed a soft, black cloth bag.

Returning to his desk, he pulled on the draw string of the bag and removed the Arabian dagger which he first saw in the Museum of Iraq in 2003. It was one of a pair. The silver hilt shone from the numerous times he had buffed it with the soft cloth. His fingers moved slowly along the blade, feeling the cold, sharp Damascus steel, until they reached the grip. He fondled the silver handle then moved his forefinger to the red ruby worked into its hilt and softly circled it with his fingertip. As he did so, he felt the khanjar speak to him: '*You should have stayed home, but you came. You should have left me in the Middle East where I belong.*'

The office door opened, and his son entered.

'Still got that dagger?' I thought you would have got rid of it a long time ago,' said John Jr. 'Why don't you sell it to Richard? He always wanted a matching pair.'

'One day, I will. Not yet,' he said, as he slipped the dagger into its sheath and placed it in the black cloth bag. What do you want?'

'You okay with the FBI agents coming to the office?'

John Tomlin expelled air. 'No, I'm not okay.'

His son gazed at him without speaking then gave a slight shrug of his shoulders and turned towards the door.

'JJ, what happened to you in Afghanistan?'

John Jr stopped, slowly turned, and stared. Stillness suffocated the room.

'What happened to me? Perhaps I should ask you the same question. What happened to you? You left us with Mum to go to Iraq.'

'You know why I went. Your Mum left me for Peter.'

'Your boss was a prick. You could have stayed home and looked after me and Susan.'

'I thought that you wanted to be with your mother.'

'Mum told you that. You didn't ask me what I wanted.'

'I'm not sure that is what you wanted.'

JJ stabbed his finger aggressively towards his father. 'Don't tell me what I did or didn't want to do. You wouldn't have a clue. You were never home.'

John Jr stormed from the office, slamming doors behind him. A motor screamed and tyres spun on the asphalt. And then there was silence.

27

APRIL 2003

Volunteering for Iraq after the completion of the second Gulf War was a no-brainer for John Tomlin. It was the only way that he was going to get back on his feet. He had just been through a messy divorce after discovering that his stateside boss had been screwing his wife for six months. Naturally, the kids stayed with their Mum, so she ended up with the house and two thirds of his salary, which she would keep receiving until Susan and John Junior were eighteen.

The posting was easy after his last assignment in Afghanistan. Afghanistan's capital, Kabul, was a shithole. The Iraqi hotel in Baghdad that had been taken over by the CIA was comfortable, and most people welcomed their presence. Saddam Hussein's forces had been beaten and the secret police and military command disbanded. Unfortunately, the victory party had turned into a hangover within three months. Law and order ceased. The strong planning that occurred for the invasion of Iraq stopped at the end of fighting. The three main rival factions in Iraq, the Shiites, Sunnis, and Kurds, were freed from Hussein's brutal control. They created militias to protect their people, and tribal leaders created paramilitary forces to loot and take property to increase their power. Civil war had broken out across the country and looting was rife.

The National Museum of Iraq was a prime target. Initially, it was opportunistic looting. But it became more organised. Staff were quickly overwhelmed and, as there were no military or police from Iraq functioning, American soldiers were tasked to guard the museum. John Tomlin was asked to assess the situation and prepare a report for Washington.

Tomlin was angry. 'You want me to go to the museum and count statues. Is that it?' He knew he was out of line but at that time in his life, he didn't care. Baghdad was turning into another Kabul.

'John, just do it,' said his frustrated boss.

'A high-level intelligence task for a veteran operative,' he replied sarcastically.

His army driver drove the Hummer to the front of the museum where he spoke to a young private.

'Who's in charge here?

'Sergeant Perez, Sir.'

Tomlin smiled to himself. Every private in Iraq called him 'Sir'. They did the same to anyone who looked over thirty.

'We just got here, Sir' said the private. 'He's taken the rest of the platoon for a recce around the building.'

'Thank you, private.' He moved to the large front gates of the museum, but they were still locked. He moved around the corner and saw two uprights in the metal fence had been forced apart. There was enough room to allow a young, skinny body to push through. He walked back to the front of the museum to find Sergeant Perez had just returned.

John Tomlin introduced himself. 'Tomlin, CIA. I've been told to get my arse down here to see what's going on.'

'Same here. I've got some of the most junior soldiers in this man's army, so we've got the job to guard a fucking museum. I posted the rest of my squad around the perimeter. So now it's hurry up and wait until we get further orders.'

'What's round the back?

'Fencing all the way round, but the rear gates have been taken off their hinges. A bit of cutting with an oxy torch, but most of the cutting has been done with a large angle grinder, I reckon.'

'Did they get inside?'

'Did they get inside? Oh yeh. There's a shipping container on a truck parked by the back roller door. It's full of stuff. One of my guys saw someone running away as we turned the corner but didn't know what to do. Couldn't tell if he was a bad guy or just a scared civi. The guy wasn't armed, so he fired a warning shot over his head.'

'Alright, can I have one of your guys to take me there?

'Sure, but he comes straight back. I need him here.'

Around the back, Tomlin saw the truck and shipping container backed close to an open roller door with a forklift sitting nearby. A quick look in the container showed statues and rock carvings of all sizes. A metal trunk sat in the opening of the container and looked like it was the last thing to be loaded. Sergeant Perez's section must have arrived just before they were about to leave with the loot.

Inside the large building, Tomlin saw open and empty glass cases, statues missing from their stands and some discarded Iraqi military uniforms.

The building was huge. He realised that figuring out what was missing would take months, especially as the museum staff had disappeared when the fighting reached Baghdad.

He reported back to HQ and came back the next day with a cameraman to start itemising the number of empty cabinets. Walking past the shipping container, he decided to look in the metal trunk. It intrigued him. He opened it to find a dozen statuettes. Most were stone, but some were carved from ivory, and some were made from bronze. Below the statuettes was jewellery, partly covering a dozen Arabian daggers. A wrapped cloth was at the very bottom of the trunk. John Tomlin slowly unwrapped the cloth and discovered two matching khanjars, one slightly larger than the other. He held one in each hand and stared at the daggers. A red ruby in the hilt of each stared back at him. The large, curved blades were sharp. The leather sheaths, with Arabic symbols the full length, were dressed in silver and curved to fit the blades. He guessed the knives would be worth thousands of dollars but knew the black market would only pay half that price.

'They're beautiful,' he said to his driver, as both stood staring at the two khanjars. He looked at them for a while longer, before saying, 'Okay, let's put the trunk in the Hummer. This stuff will go missing if we leave it here.'

They struggled with the weight of the metal box and contents but managed to lift it over the high sides of their vehicle.

Back in his hotel room, John Tomlin felt the matching daggers with his fingers. He was unable to take his eyes off them.

28

As Bec approached Jessica White's office, she could see Robert Blum was with her. Bec knocked, and Jessica waved her and Musa in.

'Jessica and I have a meeting in the executive conference room tomorrow,' said Blum. 'You'll be coming with us. The meeting starts at ten. I'll be giving a briefing and Bec, you'll respond if Jessica and I need any details filled in.'

'Yes sir.'

'The Associate Deputy Director from the Intelligence Branch is flying in from Washington. He wants to be briefed about the bombing and how far we've got with the investigation. Obviously, many people are watching what we're doing. There's a lot of interest in the case. Law enforcement agencies all over the world are watching how the investigation is progressing, and the director is asking for daily briefings. So, how is it going with your suspect?'

'We've set up phone surveillance. His movements and his calls are being monitored. Voice recognition is transcribing the phone calls, but things slow down when he speaks Arabic and some Mandarin.'

'Who's he talking to when he speaks Mandarin?'

'He has a contact at the Chinese Consulate in New York,

but we haven't identified who it is.'

'What about the calls in Arabic?

'He's speaking to his father, as well as his wife and children in Gaza.'

'What's his motive for doing the bombing?'

'Musa and I have a theory about a possible motive, and it fits with someone like Shehadeh.'

'What have you got?' asked Blum.

'From what we understand, he's a strong, passionate supporter of the Palestinian cause. He's an engineer, so he has the intelligence to make a bomb. Twelve months ago, he gave a media interview to a Palestinian television station complaining about the western world not helping with the lack of clean drinking water in Palestine.'

'And?'

'We don't think it was a serious attempt to take out the dam wall. The bombing may have been designed to bring the world's attention to the plight of the Palestinian people.' Bec paused. 'It could be a statement about water.'

'Trying to bring attention to the plight of the Palestinian people with their lack of water. Is that it?'

'The Popular Front for the Liberation of Palestine used that tactic with aircraft hijackings that started in the late sixties. They wanted to raise the world's awareness of problems in that country. Black September did it at the Munich Olympics in 1972, when they wanted political prisoners released.'

'What about help? He couldn't do it by himself.'

'His recent cell calls and emails were to colleagues and students at Columbia University or to the Chinese embassy here in New York. So, we need to go further back. That's going to take time but we're pushing things along as quickly as we can.'

Blum nodded thoughtfully. 'Okay. I'll see you both tomorrow in the conference room.'

29

Robert Blum was seated at the top of the table in the conference room when Jessica, Bec and Musa were called in to join the meeting. On his right was a younger man with glasses. Bec saw the FBI pin in the left lapel of his coat and assumed he was the Associate Deputy Director from the Intelligence Branch. Next to him was a bigger man. There were no introductions, which Bec thought unusual.

Jessica White delivered a presentation very similar to the one she gave immediately after the bombing, but this time extra details about the materials used in the bomb were provided. The presence of dichloroacetylene, which the laboratory felt increased the force of the explosion, was mentioned for the first time outside of the small group of investigators and explosive experts. She also mentioned the problem with transcribing telephone calls where Arabic and Mandarin were spoken.

'We may be able to assist there if you get bogged down,' the Associate Deputy Director from the Intelligence Branch said.

'Thank you, sir,' Jessica responded, before continuing. 'It's likely that more than one person was involved. As we know, that was the case with the Oklahoma City bombing.

One offender drove the truck with the explosives and one other assisted driving the getaway vehicle. Another two helped make the bomb. We feel that at least two people were involved in the Kensico bombing, but probably more.'

'What about the girl? Has she been identified?' said the executive from the Intelligence Branch.

'Not for certain,' said Bec. 'We've narrowed it down to two possibilities. Rosa Flores or Lucy Donaldson. We have no record of either of them. We're following up on that now.'

Robert Blum looked at the big man sitting opposite her. The man moved uncomfortably in his seat and coughed before speaking.

'Perhaps it's time I said a few words. My name is Tony Flores.' A slight South American accent permeated his voice when he introduced himself. 'I am an Operations Officer for the Central Intelligence Agency stationed here in New York. Rosa Flores is my daughter. She is an intern with the CIA, and she is studying at Columbia University.'

A stunned silence blanketed the room. Bec thought she would have heard a pin drop, even if it fell onto the plush carpet of Robert Blum's conference room.

Tony Flores quickly continued. 'Nasir Shehadeh came to our attention when he received publicity in Palestine. He was granted a scholarship to study engineering at the University of Science and Technology in Beijing. There was nothing unusual with that. China has been extending its influence in the Middle East for some time. The only notable aspect was that Shehadeh's grandfather was well known as someone who fought against the early Israeli settlements in the 1930s.'

'What about his father?' asked Bec.

'His father was a teacher. There is no information to say he was involved in Palestinian politics. His son, Nasir, trained with the Palestinian National Security Forces as a teenager but left the security forces to study at Cairo university. He completed his engineering degree there. Anyway, Shehadeh was offered a place to study in Beijing. He completed his Doctorate in Civil Engineering. He received some publicity back in Palestine when he was working in a minor role on the Three Gorges Dam project in China.'

Tony Flores drank some water before resuming.

'His media profile rose when he returned to Palestine and started talking to the political parties in the Palestinian territories about a large-scale saltwater desalination plant for Gaza and the West Bank. That publicity raised his profile in the Agency.'

'Do we know why he came to America?' asked Blum.

'We're not sure. His application to enter Columbia University mentioned studying tunnelling techniques and membranes to desalinate sea water. We are not convinced, however, that it is the real reason. His studies in China would have given him sufficient knowledge for his role with the proposed Chinese desalination plant and pipeline.'

'I see.'

'For the Chinese, the desalination plant is not the main game. They want a presence in the Sinai near the Suez Canal to protect their sea routes to Europe. They have a safe harbour and a base in Djibouti on the Horn of Africa. They can protect their shipping entering the southern entrance to the Suez Canal from there. The desalination plant gives them a reason to have a base near the northern entrance to the canal. It is all part of President Xi's Belt and Road

Initiative to increase and protect their trade routes. Also, the Egyptians have an excuse to let the Chinese have a presence in their country. So, in summary, we think Shehadeh may be a front for the Chinese.' Tony Flores smiled. 'That was a long way of saying the Agency doesn't know why Shehadeh has come to America other than trying to raise the profile of his project.'

Blum nodded. 'Tony, perhaps you can give us what information you can about Rosa?'

'Yes, that's become awkward. My daughter is studying computer engineering at Columbia. She lives at home, and during semester breaks she works as an intern at our New York office. She works on low security information. Rosa saw Shehadeh's file as a part of her duties. His file had a low security classification at the time. She saw that his class fitted with her program, and so she signed on for Middle Eastern Studies without telling anyone.'

Robert Blum clasped his hands on the polished table but didn't say anything.

Tony Flores resumed. 'It doesn't stop there. It seems that my daughter has become friendly with Lucy Donaldson.'

'Does the Agency know much about this Lucy Donaldson?' asked Blum.

'Oh yes, we know a lot about her. She's the daughter of Senator Debra Donaldson who sits on the Senate Foreign Relations Committee. The Senator takes an active interest in Middle Eastern affairs and ...' Flores checked he had everyone's attention. 'This information is only for people in this room. The Senator is considered a strong supporter of Palestine.'

30

Paul Shehadeh had spent the morning in his office. He closed his laptop and moved outside. Things had settled down at the university, and after his visit to Van Cortlandt Park with Lucy, he was confident of her support and a future possible meeting with her mother, Senator Donaldson. He was unsure about Rosa. Her reason for backing out of the golf game may have been true, but he had his doubts. Breathing the fresh breeze into his lungs, he moved towards Low Memorial Library. Lucy was on the grass outside the library chatting with Rosa. He moved towards them.

'Hi, I'm going for coffee. Would you like to join me?'

'Sorry to do this to you again, Paul, but I'm taking Lucy to a shooting range. Her first time. Would you believe it?'

'Golf and now shooting.'

'I thrashed Rosa at golf,' Lucy said, 'So now Rosa wants to make it payback time at the shooting range. Why don't you come with us?' Lucy smiled, and Paul could see the sparkle in her eyes. 'Rosa can introduce both of us to a firing range.'

'That would be interesting,' Paul answered. 'I haven't fired a gun for a long time.'

'So, why not come?'

'Let's see if Lucy enjoys the visit first.' said Rosa, quickly.

'No, I insist,' said Lucy. 'Come with us. I'm going to borrow Mum's car. We're going to a place in New Jersey where you don't need a permit; not like New York. But you'll need to bring your passport.'

'It does sound more appealing than spending the afternoon in the office,' said Paul, concentrating on Lucy and trying to ignore Rosa's lack of warmth towards him.

'Alright, we'll see you here on Amsterdam in an hour. I'm going to get Mum's car.'

'Okay, why not?'

'Don't forget your passport.'

An hour and a quarter later, Lucy pulled over to the kerb in a silver-coloured Mercedes E200. Rosa hopped in the rear and allowed Paul to sit in the front passenger seat. Within fifteen minutes, they were across the George Washington Bridge and moving from Interstate 95 onto I-80 W towards Paterson. They checked into the indoor firing range forty-five minutes later.

The instructor was standing at a glass covered counter that held about fifty handguns. About forty rifles and shotguns were mounted on the wall behind him.

'Hi Luke,' said Rosa.

'Hi Rosa. I saw your name on the bookings. Welcome back.'

'I said I'd come back with this lady. And I brought a

new customer for you.' She gave a broad smile to the handsome instructor.

Paul Shehadeh stood back as Lucy and Rosa presented their driving licences. Paul then showed his passport, which Luke photocopied.

Rosa had fired a pistol previously and wanted to try a Heckler and Koch sub-machine gun. The instructor raised his eyebrows dramatically, flirting with Rosa. Lucy said that she wanted to try a handgun.

'What about you Paul?' he asked.

'My grandfather taught me to shoot. He had an old 303 rifle. I was reading on the internet about BMG fifty cal sniper rifles. Do have one of those?'

'Fifty cal, that's serious. You'll need to find an outside range for one of those. Indoor ranges are not suitable. What about the Heckler and Koch? We'll try Lucy with a Glock, and then all of you can shoot a Heckler and Koch MP5. Will that work? The instructor looked around to check they were all in agreement. 'Okay, Rosa, do you want to start while Paul and Lucy watch the safety video?'

'Why don't we stay with one another and shoot together,' said Paul. 'You can grab a coffee while Lucy and I watch the video.'

Thirty minutes later, they entered the twenty-five-yard range and Luke introduced Lucy to a Glock 19 pistol. Lucy tried shooting the handgun with one hand, but her bullets missed or hit the left side of the target. Luke told her she was snatching rather than squeezing the trigger.

'Let me show you a two-handed grip,' said Paul.

He put his arms around her and demonstrated how to take the weight of the weapon in two hands and how she should stand with her feet apart and her left foot slightly in front of her right.

'Well done,' said Paul, after her first three bullets hit the target. 'When I fired a Glock for the first time, I didn't do that well.'

'You've fired a Glock?' asked Rosa.

'Yes, a colleague and I fired one when we flew to Phuket in Thailand while we were studying in China.'

Lucy was disappointed. 'I thought I'd be better.'

'Just remember,' said Paul, 'always use a two-handed grip.'

Luke brought the sub-machine gun over to them. 'Alright, why don't you have a go with this. Let's see who handles it best.'

Luke gave the handling procedure for the short-barrelled weapon, and they moved back to their firing positions in the twenty-five-yard range. The curved magazine held fifteen rounds. Rosa fired first. She set the lever to single shot and fired three rounds into the target from a distance of ten yards. She then placed the firing action to automatic and blew holes in the target with four bursts of automatic fire. She checked the action and magazine to ensure that it was empty.

'Nice one, Rosa,' said Luke.

'You've done it before,' said Paul.

'I haven't fired a Heckler and Koch. But Dad let me shoot an Uzi once.'

'Okay Lucy. Your turn,' said Paul.

Luke set up the new target and watched carefully as Lucy prepared to shoot. Paul saw she was nervous. Lucy missed the target with her first two single shots.

'Just relax,' said Paul. 'Take a few deep breaths, and then hold your breath when you pull the trigger.'

Lucy's next shots hit the target.

'Okay,' said Luke 'Now try a try a burst of automatic fire. Just three bullets.'

The barrel lifted as a burst of six rounds blasted from the gun, and Lucy missed the target. Luke encouraged her to relax and make sure she held the front hand grip firmly and leant forward, so the barrel didn't lift as she fired in automatic mode. Two bullets from Lucy's remaining burst of automatic fire hit the target.

Lucy's face was flushed. She wiped her sweating hands on her pants. 'I don't think guns are for me.'

Paul Shehadeh took his place at the firing point. All his single shots formed a close group of holes in the target. He then fired four bursts of automatic fire, emptying the magazine and ripping holes in the target.

'Wow,' said Lucy.

'Action man,' said Rosa, taking a long look at him. 'Not just a university lecturer.'

31

Paul Shehadeh caught Lucy's eye as she and Rosa were stuffing their backpacks before leaving the classroom. As they moved to the front of the room, he moved towards them.

'Lucy, I am giving a talk to a group called Americans for Palestine on Thursday night about my Living Water project. Would you like to come?'

'Who belongs to Americans for Palestine?' asked Rosa.

'Americans who support Palestine, of course. Different backgrounds. Most are Palestinians who live in America or are American citizens. But others are civil rights lawyers, academics or people interested in human rights.'

Lucy looked around and saw that all other students had left the room 'But what about the university ban? I don't want you getting into trouble.'

'Your mother hasn't agreed to see me yet, so I need to promote my project. I need to speak to others to raise support for it. It should be alright. It's a group that already knows about the project. They just want to hear the details.'

'Mum says the Chinese are funding it. So, why do you need support from Americans?'

Shehadeh frowned and lowered his voice. 'Please keep this to yourselves. The simple fact is, I don't trust the Chinese.'

'Why?

'What if they build their base with a desalination plant in the Sinai and stop there, and no water pipeline into Gaza is ever built. They can say the desalination plant is for the Egyptians. That alone would justify their base. I'm trying to keep my options open with my side of the project. If the Chinese don't keep their word, I need America to put pressure on the Chinese. That's why I'm in America. And that, Lucy, is why I need to speak with your mother.'

Rosa just stared at him. He wasn't sure if she believed his story. But Lucy gave a relaxed nod. It was all he needed.

32

Paul met Lucy and Rosa at Max Caffe on Amsterdam Avenue for a meal before heading to the meeting at Americans for Palestine. While they waited for their mains, they shared three serves of antipasto.

'Thanks for joining me,' said Paul, between mouthfuls of grilled aubergine.

'Are you sure you should be doing this?' asked Lucy.

'I can't just hang around waiting. I've got to do something.'

Lucy nodded and then went back to ploughing through the cheese plate.

Half an hour before the meeting, they left the restaurant. Rosa had remained quiet throughout the meal and had left most of her beet salad. Paul wondered why she had chosen to join them.

They walked along W 124th St and headed towards Harlem. After three blocks, they entered an old, five-storey red brick building near the Greater Refuge Temple. The directory showed Americans for Palestine occupying the second floor. They climbed the stairs and entered a reception area before moving straight into a meeting room. There were about fifty chairs arranged theatre style in the room.

Paul Shehadeh acknowledged a wave from a small, dark-haired man at the front of the room and started to walk towards him.

Rosa grabbed Lucy's arm and said to Paul. 'Lucy and I will sit at the back.'

'Come to the front. I'll introduce you to Yashsha.'

'Okay,' said Lucy. 'We'll sit at the front. We should show our support.'

Yashsha al Fulan opened the meeting after introducing himself as the spokesperson for Americans for Palestine to the twenty people who were present.

'Thank you all for coming. Tonight, we are going to hear from Dr Nasir Shehadeh, a graduate from the University of Cairo and the prestigious University of Science and Technology in Beijing. He is currently at Columbia and is here tonight to talk about an important water project for Palestine.' Al Fulan gave a small bow to Lucy and Rosa, who were both sitting next to Paul in the front row, and then continued.

'But since we have a couple of guests in the room, I will say a few words before I invite him to talk to you.'

'Jewish people had been migrating to Palestine for decades prior to 1948. In those years, they were the minority.'

He paused.

'But on May 15 of that year, the State of Israel came into existence. The Jewish people celebrate that day, but Palestinians call it the Great Catastrophe. And now, more and more immigrants are entering the State of Israel and Palestinians are in the minority.'

Another pause.

'Israel has a population of over eight million people.

They outnumber the six million Palestinians who live in the West Bank, Gaza and Israel. We know many Palestinian live in appalling conditions, and their water supply is inadequate. The United Nations considers much of the water used by Palestinians to be unfit for human consumption.'

Paul could see Lucy nodding as al Fulan went through his key points.

'Now, these truths provide the segue for our guest speaker, Dr Nasir Shehadeh, to come forward and talk about his project, which he calls Living Water. An appropriate name.'

Shehadeh stood and thanked al Fulan for his introduction and for the opportunity to speak. Then, over the next forty-five minutes, he outlined his project. When he'd finished, he offered to answer any questions.

An elderly Middle Eastern woman stood. 'Dr Shehadeh, I welcome your initiative, but do you really believe that a pipeline from Gaza to the West Bank is possible? The Israelis will not let it happen.'

Paul nodded towards the woman and thought about his answer. The woman sat down and waited.

'In nineteen sixty-three, the American civil rights leader Martin Luther King said he had a dream. It was a difficult time for black people in America. Today, Palestinians face difficult times. We have been facing them for years. We've fought wars to keep our land. My grandfather fought the settlers decades ago, but they still come.'

Paul took a deep breath.

'My father has a dream for Palestine. Fighting does not exist in his dream. His vision involves education and persuasion. We need to persuade the Israelis of the benefits of Living Water.'

You can't persuade the Israelis,' said the woman.

'Perhaps not. But then, let's persuade the Americans of the benefits of Living Water. I am following my father's ideas. My father wants a better way, a different way from my grandfather. That is why I'm in America.'

He was pleased to see the woman nod, perhaps not in agreement but accepting that he had a point to consider.

He looked around to see if there were any more questions. He saw Rosa was heading for the door. Lucy mouthed 'sorry' and followed her. Paul was about to wrap up, but a young man called out.

'If you build your pipeline from Gaza into the West Bank, Israeli extremists will sabotage it.'

'Yes, they will. But I want to put my pipeline underground. Trenching and back fill will protect it from all but the most determined extremists.'

'What about attacks from Israeli aircraft or artillery shells?'

'I've considered that. Trenching and backfill would normally be sufficient, but some tunnel boring and underground storage tanks will be needed as we get closer to the West Bank.'

The room was silent. Some from the audience were starting to lift their bags from the floor.

Al Fulan stood up. 'No more questions, then? No? Okay. Thank you everyone for coming. Please thank Dr Shehadeh for his presentation. It's a very exciting project for Palestine.'

Most of the audience moved from the room, leaving a small group standing in the aisle talking excitedly amongst themselves.

'Paul, your project opens many exciting possibilities,' said al Fulan. 'Clean drinking water, but also the possibility for greater independence for Palestine.'

'Yes. My father is very pleased with what I'm trying to do.'

'He would be very proud. Tell me, will the Chinese keep their word?'

'I believe so. They are very keen to have a presence in the Middle East. But we need the support of influential Americans to make sure it happens. If the Chinese go back on their word, America can encourage countries in the West to put pressure on them to complete the project.'

Paul thanked al Fulan and packed his laptop into his backpack. He wondered if news of the talk would filter back to the university. The ban on talking about the project was still in place. He hoped the risk had been worth it. He needed support.

33

Lucy slipped her arm around Rosa as they walked back towards Columbia University from the Americans for Palestine meeting. 'Isn't he wonderful?' she said.

Lucy felt Rosa stiffen.

'He's not all that he seems.'

'What do you mean?' asked Lucy looking at Rosa.

'He's being too friendly. I wonder if he's using you to get to your mother. Sorry, but I had to say it.'

'Paul's not like that.'

'You know, said Rosa, 'there's always two sides to a story. Paul just talks about how bad it is for Palestinians.'

'It's not just Paul. The UN says they don't have enough clean water.'

'Lucy, it's not just the water issue. What about Israelis trying to live their lives when the Palestinians are firing rockets at them. What about their rights?

'The Palestinians are fighting for their land. Israeli settlements are growing all the time.'

Rosa stopped and turned to her. 'My cousin's mother is Jewish. Her father was murdered by the Nazis, and her mother did forced labour in a concentration camp. Paul might be trying to do important things, but remember there are two sides to the story.'

'Yes, but that was over fifty years ago. Now, it's Palestinians being persecuted.'

'Does Paul talk about the suicide bombings by Palestinians? No. Does he talk about Hamas getting young boys to throw stones at Israelis and then paying compensation to the families when the boys are killed or wounded?'

'But Rosa, Israelis of all people should know what it feels like being wronged. Paul's trying to help his people. He needs our support.'

Rosa shook her head and slipped from Lucy's arm. 'I've got to go. Bye.' She strode across the road without looking back.

Lucy stood on the pavement and watched Rosa disappear, wondering what had got into her friend. She hadn't realised Rosa was so against Paul. She turned around thinking she might go back to him but changed her mind and hurried off to the parking garage where she'd left her mother's car. After the argument with Rosa, she wanted to get home.

34

Lucy was enjoying the sun that was shining through the window as she waited for her mother to join her at the breakfast table, the family's favourite place on weekends. She was back from Washington, and Lucy thought it could be an ideal time to speak with her about Shehadeh. When her mother came into the room, Lucy jumped up and made her toast and coffee, then waited until she'd finished eating and was sipping her coffee and reading the morning news on her iPad.

'Mum, can't you do something for Palestine?'

Debra Donaldson looked up from her coffee. 'What exactly do you want me to do for Palestine?'

'Can't we help get water for Palestine? What if America supported Paul Shehadeh's pipeline project?'

'I see, Shehadeh's scheme.' A frown formed on her forehead. 'You know it's being funded by the Chinese. They won't want American involvement.'

'I know. But Paul thinks the Chinese will put the pipeline from Egypt into Gaza, but the Israelis won't allow it to cross the land they are occupying. He says the Israelis won't let it continue to the West Bank, and the Chinese will go along with that.'

'He's probably right.'

'He spoke about his project at a meeting I went to. He was brilliant. We should do something. Can't you speak to the committee you work on? Or the President? America should pressure the Israelis to let it happen.'

Lucy saw her mother eyeballing her. 'When did he speak?'

'A couple of days ago. Americans for Palestine. He was the guest speaker.'

'You were at the meeting?'

Lucy thought it best not to say that Paul had invited her, and they were together. 'Yes, I went with Rosa.'

'I was under the impression he had been requested not to speak about his project.'

'Really?' said Lucy, not admitting that she knew about the ban.

'You know that your presence at the meeting could embarrass me? We've talked about this sort of thing. What you do can cause problems for me. You know that.'

'You're saying I can't have a life and a view about what is happening in the world. Is that it?'

'No. I'm asking you to be careful, that's all. Now, these ideas you have, are they your own or is Shehadeh asking you to speak to me?'

'I'm not a child. It's my idea to speak to you. I can think, you know. But what if he did? It's the right thing to do.'

Her mother nodded. 'The President has many issues to consider before telling the Israelis to let the Chinese build a water pipeline across their land.'

Lucy raised her voice. 'Mum, it's not their land. It's Palestinian land, and they need our support. What's the point of being a senator if you can't influence important projects like this?'

'Do you want to help the Palestinian people or Shehadeh?' Debra Donaldson asked quietly.

'Mum, don't twist things around. The Israelis are bullies.'

'Lucy, the situation in the Middle East is complicated. Please don't be naïve.'

Lucy's frustration spilled over into anger. She stormed from the house, slamming the front door behind her, and walked towards the East River, passing the rows of brownstone homes and consulates in Murray Hill. By the time she reached the plaza of the United Nations Building and had found a seat, she'd worked out her next move: her mother wouldn't budge, but she could talk to her stepfather. That might work.

35

John Tomlin Jr drove into the parking lot of Industrial Chemical Supplies. Beside him, in the passenger seat, was Bobby Brown, the storeman. They had been away from the warehouse all morning. As his father strode quickly towards them, JJ whispered to Bobby.

'Keep your mouth shut.'

He opened the driver's door and stepped out.

'Where have you been?'

They were the first words he'd heard from his father since the FBI visit to the warehouse.

'None of your business.'

'It is my business. I'm your father, and you work for me. Bobby was needed in the warehouse.'

'Moses owns it, and he asked us to meet him.'

'What about? He didn't say anything to me.'

'That's between Richard and me.'

'JJ——'

'Don't hold your hand out to me. It's too late now.'

He watched his father turn and shuffle back towards the warehouse. He looked like an old man. Any influence his father possessed over him had evaporated.

JJ saw Bobby staring at him. 'If the old man says

anything to you, keep your mouth shut. Got it?'

'Sure, JJ. I won't say nothin.'

When his father appeared from his office an hour later, his eyes were swollen and red.

'JJ, I want to know why you were discharged from the military.'

'Why?'

'You've changed. You were happy in the military, but ever since you came home you've been angry.'

'You were in the CIA. Did you know that I applied for the CIA? I wanted to be like you. Did you know that?'

'No, I didn't know. You never told me.'

JJ stared hard at his father, the anger building. Thinking of the past always fuelled the anger in him.

'You were always away,' he said. 'We never talked.'

'Yes, I know. I'm sorry. But what about leaving the military? Why were you discharged from the military?'

'Let me finish. When the CIA knocked me back, I joined the infantry. I wanted to serve my country. They taught me to kill, and I was good. So, they promoted to me to corporal. Then I taught new soldiers to kill. I blooded them. And everything was going just fine.'

JJ stared at his father.

'And you know what happened? Bobby was to make his first kill, but he was nervous. I was encouraging him. I told him to take the shot. But the hadji he killed was a civilian.' JJ shook his head. 'Would you believe it?'

'Don't call them hadjis. They're people like you and me.'

'I'll call them what I like. They want to kill us.'

'Not all of them,' his father said quietly.

'And you know what the military did to me? You know what they did? They spat me out. I was a good soldier, but they didn't want me anymore.'

JJ moved towards his father and stabbed his finger into his chest. 'Just–like–you–didn't–want–me.'

'JJ, that's not true.'

JJ's anger rose another notch. His face distorted with rage and his voice strained. 'Don't start. Just, don't start. I'll show you. I'll show all of you.'

36

A shipment of chemicals arrived, and JJ checked the contents as Bobby Brown worked the forklift, storing them in neat rows in the warehouse. When he returned to the office, the phone was ringing.

'Industrial Chemical Supplies.'

'JJ, it's Richard Moses.'

'Hi, Richard.'

'Your father rang me. Is he at the warehouse?'

'Yeah. Why?'

'Is he alright?'

'He's a bit down, but he'll be okay.'

'Can you check on him? He sounded really down. I've never heard him like that.'

'I'm sure he's fine.'

'JJ, just check. Something's up.'

'Okay. I'll ring you back.'

JJ went to his father's office and knocked on the door.

'Dad?'

There was no response from his father, so he tried the handle. The door was locked.

'Dad, you okay?'

He listened, but there was no answer. He walked over to

the entrance of the office building and looked out. His father's car was still parked in its normal position. Frowning, he went over to the warehouse where Bobby was storing containers of chemicals into their safe storages.

'You seen Dad?'

'I thought he was in his office. Everything okay?'

'Yeh, yeh. No problem.'

JJ returned to his father's office and banged on the door.

'Dad, open the door.'

No answer.

'Dad, can you hear me?'

He stepped backed and kicked out, hitting the door near the handle. The door flung open, and JJ stepped into the office. There was no sign of his father, but JJ could hear the shower going in the adjacent bathroom. He crossed the room and opened the unlocked door. His father was sitting slumped in the shower dressed in his T shirt and boxer shorts.

'Dad!'

Water from the shower ran red down the drain. There were deep cuts across his father's wrists, but little blood was coming from the arteries.

'Fuck.'

He ran to his father and dragged him from under the shower. The jewelled Arabian dagger fell from his father's lap onto the floor of the shower, the blood on its blade the colour of the ruby in its handle.

'You silly prick,' he said, without any real emotion. He grabbed two towels to put pressure on the wounds, but blood was no longer pumping from them. Looking at his father's face, he knew he was dead.

JJ sat back and stared at his body. The anger that always inhabited him barely existed at that moment. He looked over at the dagger on the floor of the shower cubicle and stared as water cleansed his father's blood from its curved blade.

After a few minutes, JJ turned off the water, picked up the dagger and moved into his father's office. No blood was visible, but it was still wet. He cautiously wiped the moisture from it and held the dagger in the light streaming through the office window. He studied it closely. No blood or moisture could be seen. He eased the blade into its sheath and placed the dagger into its black cloth bag and returned it to his father's safe in the storeroom.

JJ returned to the office and sat in his father's chair, swivelling in it before punching a speed dial on his cell phone.

'He's dead,' he said abruptly when Richard Moses answered.

'What happened?'

'Killed himself. Slit his wrists in the shower with that dagger you always wanted.'

Moses did not reply for a moment before asking, 'What are you going to do?'

'Leave it with me. I'll talk to you later.'

JJ moved to the small kitchen across the passage and took a boning knife from the drawer. He returned to the bathroom and kneeled beside his father. He slowly pulled the blade of the knife through each cut in his father's wrists and placed the knife on the floor. He looked around the bathroom then returned to his father's desk.

My desk, he thought, before reaching for his cell phone and dialling 911.

37

John Tomlin Jr sat with Bobby Brown in the front row of the chapel at the funeral home in East Main Street, Port Jervis. Ten people were present. Three were associates who did business with Industrial Chemical Supplies. They sat in the chairs behind JJ. Richard Moses sat at the back. The other four were the owners and employees of the funeral home. His sister did not attend the funeral of her father. She lived close to her mother on the West Coast.

The closed coffin was guarded by two stands of flowers sitting on pedestals. After the funeral director said a few words from the podium about John Tomlin living a good life that ended far too early, the unadorned coffin slid back behind the heavy curtains at the front of the chapel and disappeared.

After the short observance, JJ moved to the three associates of the business and spoke with them until they finished their coffee and cake and left. Half an hour later, he walked out with Bobby. Richard Moses was waiting in his white Lexus. He got out of his car when he saw them.

'Let's take a walk.'

JJ looked at Bobby. 'Wait for me in the car.'

Moses and JJ walked to the playing fields of Port Jervis Middle School.

'I'm sorry about your dad.'

JJ shrugged his shoulders. 'Dad was losing it. Every day, he took that dagger from his safe and played with it. He should've sold it to you years ago.' JJ looked at the grey sky. 'What did Dad say when he rang on the day he died?'

'He didn't talk long. He just spoke about how he'd made sure the business was in good shape and how I could deal with you from now on. He didn't sound right. That's why I rang you.'

'That's all?'

'I asked if he was alright. But he ended the call.'

JJ lit a cigarette.

'What did you say to the cops?' asked Moses.

'I told them Dad was worried about getting old but that I didn't think that things were that bad.'

'There's been no follow-up by the cops about his death?'

'The fat sergeant kept bellyaching that it was his second death that week and he was snowed under because the first one was a murder. He wasn't worried about the old man's death.'

'What did the cops do with the dagger?'

'They haven't got it.'

Moses stared at him.

JJ smiled. 'I swapped it for a kitchen knife.'

Richard Moses gave a slow nod of his head. 'Smart move. What are you going to do with it?'

'What's it worth to you?'

Moses' face became animated. His eyes shifted from JJ to distant objects, and he sucked air between his teeth several times.

'I'm sure we can come to a suitable arrangement. Where is it?'

'It's in a safe place.'

'Keep it safe. Let's talk about it when everything has settled down. You can handle things with Shehadeh?'

'I can handle things. As the old man said, you can deal with me. You won't have to go behind his back now.' JJ dragged on his cigarette. 'Dad was getting old. He worried too much.'

'What about when the FBI comes back to check on the chemicals?'

'I told you; I can handle things. The paperwork is in order.'

'Can Bobby keep his mouth shut? He worries me.'

'I'll make sure he keeps his mouth shut.'

Moses stared at him. JJ gave him a half smile.

'Okay, you're the man to do the job.'

They walked back to the funeral home. Richard Moses got into his expensive white Lexus and drove away. JJ watched him leave and walked over to his father's black BMW sedan, the last vehicle in the parking lot. He jumped into the driver's seat and felt the rich leather. He then used the controls to adjust the seat slightly. Happy that he'd got the seat position just right, he pushed the memory button, started the turbo charged motor and drove from the parking lot of the funeral home with a smile on his face.

38

John Tomlin Junior sped onto a wooded twenty-acre property, half an hour from Port Jervis. He raced the black BMW along the edge of the grass airstrip and past the aircraft hangar, then skidded to a halt near the double doors of the garage attached to the large, ranch-style home owned by Richard Moses.

Once inside the home, he went straight to the kitchen and entered the pantry. He lifted the lid from the bulk sugar container and reached in, removing a plastic bag containing a glass pipe and a smaller plastic bag holding white crystals. He then moved to the lounge and sat in a large chair facing the sixty-inch television that was mounted on the wall. After placing the bag on the low table in front of the chair, he removed the pipe and placed some crystals in the bowl and heated it. Grey fumes rose. JJ inhaled. Soon the euphoria hit, and he started to massage his crotch.

JJ woke just before dawn with a fuzzy head and furry tongue. Moving to the kitchen, he flicked the switch on the coffee machine but didn't wait for the black liquid to heat up. He poured some into a mug, added three sugars to the cold coffee and finished it in four gulps.

Back in his bedroom, JJ went into the ensuite, dropped his boxer shorts to the floor and stepped into to the shower. He turned on the cold water tap and let the water pepper his face and body. Slowly, his brain started to work again, and he allowed himself to turn on the hot water.

Revived, JJ stepped from the cubicle and towelled himself dry, looking in the mirror. He was thankful for what the army had done for his body. He was chiselled and strong from the military's physical training.

JJ dressed and went back to the kitchen. The coffee was percolating. He poured more of the black fluid into his mug, stretched and went out onto the front veranda. The sun was rising. Its rays touched the tree leaves, the green of the sugar maple and the burgundy of the red maple. The landscape was completely different from the rock and sand of Afghanistan. And there were no people around, which is what he liked: people cause problems; people ask if you are okay. The woods and isolation protected his privacy, and the property's small airstrip allowed him to fly his Acro Sport.

JJ went back inside and placed his empty coffee mug in the kitchen sink. He picked up his iPad on his way back outside and moved to the airplane hangar to the right of the house, where he kept his biplane. He punched his father's birthdate into the keypad of the access door and stepped inside. The week before he'd been slow to recover from a spin and had come close to crashing. But that was all part of the fun of aerobatics. Anyway, he'd looked at the YouTube clip a few more times since then. Today he'd be perfect.

Grabbing hold of the propeller, he lowered the nose of the plane. The tail wheel rose into the air and made it easier pulling the small plane from its hangar. The pre-flight checks didn't take long. He knew the plane and had filled the tank after the previous flight. When he pushed the starter button, the Lycoming motor burst into life, the noise from the unmuffled exhaust causing a small flock of American Redstarts to fly from nearby trees. He checked the controls while taxiing to the southern extremity of the runway. Reaching the end, he gunned the motor while pushing on the pedal that applied the brakes to the left wheel. The little plane spun around to face into the wind. Tension built slightly as he held the brakes while increasing the speed of the motor. The little plane started to rock and shake. He released the brakes, and the plane pushed forward and rose into the air when it reached fifty knots. With the wind now in his face, JJ smiled.

At three thousand feet and nearing Greenwood Lake Airport, JJ aggressively dropped the nose of the biplane and dived towards the ground. The earth rushed towards him as the airspeed increased. At two thousand feet, he pulled back the joystick to point the small plane's nose to the sky, continuing to hold it there until he was hanging upside down in the cockpit and blood was rushing to his head.

'Yeah,' he screamed, as he completed the loop. Fear and exhilaration rushed through his body, just as it had in his first engagement with the Taliban, in a barren country half a world away.

39

AFGHANISTAN 2018

John Tomlin Junior's platoon moved quietly onto high ground near the village. The young soldiers disappeared into hiding places in the rock and dirt, just as dawn was ending night. Below him, there was little movement in the rural community. As the sun rose, smoke from the mud brick homes increased, and the Afghan villagers started moving about, casually undertaking their chores.

JJ's sergeant was on his third tour. He moved amongst his young soldiers on the hill, making sure they were ready for their first action.

'Are you ready for first blood?' he said quietly into JJ's ear. 'Are you ready?'

JJ felt his fear frothing up inside. His lips and tongue were dry, and his saliva wouldn't flow. JJ nodded, worried his voice would give away his feelings. His sergeant slapped him on his back and moved to the next young infantryman along the line.

Previously, JJ had heard the sergeants talking over beers.

He had a short stint as barman in the sergeants' mess. One of the older sergeants was animated, speaking with a slur to a newly promoted sergeant. 'They're useless as tits on a bull until they get their first kill. Make sure that happens … and it's got to be done early in their tour.'

As the sun warmed his body, JJ relaxed. The Afghan village reminded him of an Indian village in Arizona that he saw as a boy. The only difference was the lack of vehicles here.

Two hours after sunrise, dust was seen in the distance. A motorbike approached the village and stopped near the door of one of the larger mud brick buildings. A man stepped from the house and said something to the Afghan who was riding the bike. The rider lifted his hand and spoke into a two-way radio.

The sergeant sidled up to JJ. 'Tomlin don't let that rider out of your sight. When I give the word to fire, you take him out. You got that?'

'Yes, sergeant.'

Half an hour later, another plume of dust was seen in the distance. The motor was heard a short time later.

'Truck, probably four in the back,' JJ heard through his headset.

JJ kept the sights of his rifle on the motorcycle rider as the vehicle stopped next to the bike. Two Afghans got out of the cabin and another four jumped from the rear of the vehicle. Four were carrying assault rifles and one was carrying a rocket propelled grenade launcher.

The rider was too far away for a head shot, so he kept the sights on his chest. He felt a strange sense of excitement, which built and built until it climaxed when he heard the voice of the platoon's lieutenant in his headset.

'Fire. Fire.'

John Tomlin Jr squeezed the trigger of his rifle and watched the bullet punch the chest of his target. The motor-cycle rider fell to the ground and didn't move: first blood.

40

JJ walked out of New York Hilton Midtown's largest event room with Richard Moses. The hotel, on Avenue of the Americas, was busy with delegates from across the world discussing water infrastructure. The lead delegate from Israel had just finished the session with his presentation about water re-use.

JJ dropped back and watched as Richard Moses mingled with the Israeli presenter and his companions. He was bored. His Dad would have loved being at the conference, but he'd rather be in his plane. He went over to the urn and made himself a coffee and then went back to his boss.

A well-dressed Chinese man approached Moses.

'Hello, Richard, can we have a chat?'

Moses looked at the man's face and quickly glanced at his name tag.

'Yes, of course. You are?'

'Hongwen, but please call me John.'

The Chinese man extended his arm for a handshake. 'Perhaps we can have a coffee?'

Moses took the man's hand and then looked at JJ. 'I'll see you back inside.'

JJ watched Hongwen guide Moses to the coffee, but

then he was distracted by the young blonde delegate from Sweden, who he'd noticed when he checked in. When he looked around again, Moses was talking with Hongwen in a quiet corner. He put down his coffee cup and returned to the conference room.

'What was that all about?' he said, when Moses joined him.

It was some time before Moses replied.

'He said we had a common problem.'

'What common problem?'

'Our friend, Shehadeh, has become an embarrassment to them,' said Moses. 'He's been talking to people about extending a water pipeline from Gaza into the West Bank.'

'So?'

'The Chinese don't want it to happen.'

'That's the problem with dealing with those people. They can't be trusted.'

'Who, the Palestinians or the Chinese?'

'Both.'

'They feel that it would be better if he doesn't return home.'

'Why don't they deal with him?' said JJ. 'I've done enough.'

'If you're worried about doing more, so be it.'

'I don't worry about anything.'

'Yes, I believe you. Your father was the complete opposite. He'd have an ulcer by now. Anyway, it seems the Chinese are about to start building their base in the Sinai.'

'I've done everything you've asked. I even attended classes at Columbia for you. Me, attending classes at university, now that was funny. Anyway, you got that and more.'

'Yes, my new Chinese friend said you attended some of Shehadeh's early classes.'

'You said to keep an eye on him.'

'I didn't say for you to make yourself stand out,' said Moses. 'Why did you write comments on the whiteboard?'

'Did he tell you that?'

'Yeh, he did.'

'I told you they can't be trusted.'

'Anyway, perhaps you can think of something else. This time without making it obvious.'

'Why should I?'

Richard Moses moved slightly forward and looked into his eyes. 'Because you like it. You enjoy doing these things much more than sitting in a warehouse office.'

JJ looked back at Moses and smiled.

'I suppose I do.'

41

During their lunch break, Bec and Musa jogged from their office. It was their first true lunch break since the bombing. They headed to the basketball courts at West Thames Park to shoot hoops. After fifteen minutes, both were starting to lift their heart rates, but neither had raised a sweat.

'Do you need a break?' asked Bec, after going two points ahead with a layup.

'Break? I'm just getting started.' He stepped behind the line and landed a three pointer.

'Nice one.'

Bec recovered the ball and threw it back to her partner. Musa took the ball and dribbled quickly towards her, making a feint. Bec raised her arms expecting him to shoot, but he bounced it between his legs and stepped around her. He lifted the ball into the air. It hit the backboard before dropping into the basket. It was game on.

When the alarm on Bec's watch sounded, twenty minutes later, Musa was behind.

'Time,' she said.

'Another five minutes?

'Perhaps later.' She grabbed her towel and started wiping

away the sweat. 'So, what have we got with our investigation?' she asked. 'We've got a suspect, Shehadeh, from an anonymous tip off. He has the intelligence to make a bomb and a possible motive.'

'He probably had the help of at least one other person to drive him away after the bombing,' said Musa. 'Same with stealing the garbage truck and filling it with explosives. What associates do we know about?'

'We know he's friendly with two of his students. A young woman was with him at Kensico Reservoir. From the CCTV, it looks like it was Lucy Donaldson.'

'And she's the daughter of a New York Senator. Hardly a prime suspect for helping bomb a New York reservoir, unless she's doing a Patty Hearst,' said Musa frowning. 'If he was involved, there are other people we don't know about.'

'Most likely men. Very few women have been involved with bombings in the past,' said Bec, wiping her face with her towel. 'What about his contact in the Chinese Embassy?'

'I don't know. You wouldn't think so. The Chinese want him to win over different Palestinian factions with his desalination project. What motive would the Chinese have to get involved in a bombing in America?' Musa started bouncing the ball in preparation for taking another shot. 'You know, I still think this is another pointless Middle Eastern job we've been given, Semra Bekele.' He stretched the middle syllable of Bec's last name, emphasising the Ethiopian pronunciation.

'Why are you bringing that up again?' asked Bec, with a puzzled look on her face.

'No Palestinian organisation has claimed responsibility for the bombing. If they want to raise the profile of water issues in Palestine, they would have done it by now. It hasn't happened.' Musa tried for a three pointer but missed. 'I think we've been given a bum lead.'

'Why?'

'Who knows. Perhaps someone doesn't like Shehadeh?'

Bec's anger rose. It rarely happened. 'Don't you go negative on me. Who knows why publicity hasn't happened? Something could have gone wrong. So, suck it up, princess. It's our job and we're going to do it properly.' She grabbed the ball and landed a three-point throw. 'Look, when I asked Jessica White if I could work with you, I knew it wouldn't be easy. Look at us. We're the odd couple. But I had a feeling about you when I first saw you at the gym at Quantico. You were given the nickname, Moose, for a reason. You can be tough and dangerous to the bad guys.'

'So, you wanted to work with me because I could break someone's nose?'

'It helps,' said Bec, keeping a straight face.

'Well, Jessica asked what my wife would think of me working with you.'

'Why would she ask that?'

'None of the wives want their husbands working with you. They think you're too pretty.'

'That's rubbish.'

'True. The guys just don't want to work with a woman taller than them.'

Bec broke into laughter and was rewarded with a smile from Musa. 'You and I are among the best the office has got. We've shown it separately, and we're going to prove it again with this job.' She threw him the ball. 'You're five points down.'

'Not for long,' he said, bouncing the ball as he moved back onto the court.

Musa evened the score over the next ten minutes, then Bec moved gracefully around Musa's block and dropped a layup just as the timer on her watch sounded.

'Too good,' said Musa as both agents wiped themselves down.

They jogged back to the office, but as soon as Bec sat down at her desk, she got a calendar alert on her cell phone.

'Got to go. Jessica and I have a meeting with the boss. Something about Shehadeh.'

'And leave me to push paper.'

Bec ignored Musa's comments and went to find her former partner.

'Have you discovered what this meeting is about?' she asked Jessica, when she got to her office.

'No, but we are about to find out.'

Jessica grabbed her jacket from the back of her chair and headed for the lifts. Ten floors later, they exited onto the executive floor of New York's FBI offices. Special Agent Blum's secretary ushered them into his office. CIA agent Tony Flores was already in the room.

Jessica and Bec remained standing.

'You've met Tony Flores,' said Blum. It was a statement more than a question.

'Yes sir,' replied Jessica.

'Well, it seems Tony's office has been contacted by the Vice President, Human Resources at Columbia University. Claire Conway wants to have a talk about Nasir Shehadeh. Tony felt our office should speak to Conway, especially as his daughter is attending Shehadeh's class at the university.'

Bec noticed he didn't mention she was having coffee with him, as well.

'Also, I thought it best if Bec went by herself to see the Vice President. I don't want more than one agent on the university campus. I don't want our visit to generate any interest, especially around the engineering school.'

42

Claire Conway rose to greet Bec as she entered the room. Her face was pale and drawn. Bec spoke quietly but with authority as she sat on leather seats at Conway's desk. 'I understand you contacted another agency about an issue you are trying to resolve. I believe it involves Dr Nasir Shehadeh.'

'The CIA rang and told me you would be handling this issue. Thank you for coming.'

The Vice President explained the situation with Shehadeh's project and his application to attend Columbia University.

'The university is particularly concerned that his project with the Chinese would embarrass the university if it became more widely known.'

'Could you start from the beginning and explain how he got into Columbia? What's the process?'

Claire Conway frowned. 'He came to Columbia as a post-doctoral research fellow and casual lecturer. He was qualified and the university likes to support projects that help people. Supplying clean drinking water to Palestinians falls within the university's criteria.'

'Why did you contact the CIA?'

'He was less than frank with the details of the project. His plans for a water pipeline that crossed the border between Egypt and Gaza raises concerns for the university. And his vision to continue it across Israeli land to the West Bank ... his audacity is breathtaking. The university feels that the appropriate government department should be aware of his project.'

'Did Shehadeh's application have any references? Does he know anyone in America?'

Bec noticed a hesitation.

'He has references from influential people who are members of a group called Americans for Palestine.'

'Could I have those names, please? The information will remain confidential.'

'Certainly. If you would like to wait after the meeting, my secretary will get you a copy of the files.' Conway touched the folder in front of her. 'There is something else you need to know.'

Bec waited for the Vice President to continue.

'I'm passing on this information in the strictest confidence.'

'Of course.'

'After his application arrived, I received a telephone call from a senator's office about Dr Shehadeh. One of her political operatives made it clear that the senator wanted Shehadeh to get a spot at Columbia.'

'Which senator?'

'Debra Donaldson, the senator for New York.'

'Is the senator a member of Americans for Palestine?'

'I don't know,' she snapped. 'Your office would probably have a better idea about that.'

Bec did not react.

'And …' Claire Conway put her hands on either side of her face and took a deep breath. 'His supervisor, Professor John Marshall, is the senator's husband.'

Bec was curious. 'Is that normal?'

'No. I assume it was just a coincidence. I didn't mention the phone call about Shehadeh to anyone. His qualifications and other references would get him in without any referrals.'

Claire Conway's eyes closed, and she massaged her temples. 'First COVID, then China stopping students coming to America and now this. The university can't afford any more problems.' She looked at Bec. 'Can I be candid?'

'Of course.'

'The university is keen that this matter does not receive any publicity. We are concerned that it would distress some of our benefactors.'

43

As Paul Shehadeh left his small office and walked along the corridor, he realised he was frowning. He stepped out of the building into the fresh air, hoping to clear his head. The warmth of the day lifted his spirits a little, and he tilted his head to feel the sun on his face, vaguely aware that someone was watching him. He looked around and saw a young man. He wasn't sure, but it looked like the young man who wrote on the whiteboard. He hadn't seen him since the incident and even wondered if he was a student at Columbia. So long as he didn't turn up in Middle Eastern Studies, Paul didn't really care. He had other things to think about.

He put the young man to the back of his mind and started walking to a nearby café. Recently, he'd begun to feel as if he was being followed, and so he would vary his speed. Sometimes, he would slow down as though he was window shopping. Other times, he would increase his speed or even jog and then double back. Occasionally, he would see a man or woman who he thought was watching him, but they would disappear or just walk past.

His happiness at being in America had evaporated. He was concerned about developments at the university. Nothing was straightforward anymore. The whiteboard incident had unsettled him. Then, there was the problem with his application to study at Columbia. And he had expected to be successful promoting his project, but that was going nowhere. Lucy's mother still hadn't met with him. Getting to speak with politically well-connected people about his ideas was impossible. He seemed cursed with bad luck. How can you speak with important people if you can't meet with them? Surely, Americans know, if you control a country's water you control the people.

He understood how much President Xi Jinping's expansionist policies were threatening America's place in the world and how America's political elite were working hard to counteract China's growing power. He felt Americans would resist the Chinese building a base in the Sinai, but the Chinese would still go ahead. Then, American diplomats could criticise the base as a ruse if they didn't go ahead with the pipeline. He was learning that Palestine was not high on the agenda of American politicians. He had been foolish to think otherwise. Storm clouds were building in other parts of the world.

He walked into the coffee shop in Columbia Northwest Corner Building on W 152nd Street, where he'd agreed to meet Lucy. She was sitting at a table by the window watching out for him.

'Let's sit at the back,' said Paul.

'Why don't we sit here in the sun? It's nice and warm.'

'No, let's sit at the back.'

They moved to an empty table at the rear of the coffee shop.

'Don't you want to be seen with one of your students? You know I don't mind.'

'It's not that. We can always say we're talking about an assignment.' He paused and looked around. 'I think I'm being followed.'

'Really? Who'd be following you?'

'The Israelis, the Chinese, even one of your spy agencies. I don't know.'

'Why would we be following you?' asked Lucy.

Paul looked at her. 'My sweet, sweet Lucy, sometimes I feel Americans are so naïve.'

Lucy looked shocked, but Paul noticed she recovered very quickly.

'My mother called me naïve when I was trying to help you. And now you're saying Americans are naïve. What do you mean Americans are naïve?'

'Anyone with a few brains knows America works with the Israelis. Your country supplies warplanes to Israel. Warplanes that shoot missiles at my people.'

Lucy smiled, but it wasn't her normal, soft smile that lit up her face.

'Perhaps, it's you who's naïve. All I want you to do is take me to bed.'

He tried to take her hand, realising his mistake.

'Lucy, I'm sorry. I was out of line.'

Lucy pulled her hand away. 'I've got to go. If you're being followed, I better stop seeing you. I don't want my mother to find out what I'm up to.'

Lucy picked up her backpack and swung it over one shoulder. Her blonde hair flew from the smooth, fair skin of her face. She turned towards the door and left without looking back. Paul Shehadeh closed his eyes and shook his head.

Nasir, you're an idiot.

44

The owner of the recycling depot at West Milford watched through his office window as a young man walked into his yard. He hoped it meant some business. Things were quiet, and he had bills to pay.

'Hi,' he said, as the young man entered the office.

'Hi, I was told I might be able to hire a garbage truck here. Mine has broken down, and I need to finish a job.'

'I've got a front loader you can have. Some bastard stole my side loader.'

'Too bad. You don't know who to trust these days. A front loader will do the job.'

'It'll cost you $500 a day.'

'Sure. It's got joystick controls?'

'No. You'd pay twice as much for a more modern truck. But it'll do the job. What are you picking up?'

'Some dead meat.'

The yard owner looked under his drooping eyelids at his new customer but didn't say anything. He lifted his tired, old body from his chair and walked to a small box on the wall.

'I'll get the keys and show you the truck.'

'That's alright. I know where the keys are.'

The old man stopped and slowly turned back to look at the young man and stared into the black barrel of a pistol.

45

At the start of the investigation, Bec had introduced Musa to the café on Chambers Street, which was a regular haunt of hers. She first went there when she was working with Jessica White. A coffee break allowed them to get out of the office and stretch their legs. They could disappear amongst the dark timber wainscotting at the rear of the café or grab a takeaway and walk to the Hudson River. Although, like today, Bec was more likely to drink green tea.

They were sitting in the rear corner, Musa with his usual short black, a tradition in his family, and Jessica, who had joined them to discuss the investigation. No diners were near their table, so they were able to discuss their investigation freely.

The revelation that Lucy Donaldson and Rosa Flores were students in Shehadeh's class had caused them to speculate about the relationship between Shehadeh and the two young women. Surveillance had shown the three associated more often than other students in the class.

'Now Tony Flores has told us that his daughter is one of the two young women with Shehadeh, it explains Rosa's actions,' said Bec.

'I understand he had a quiet word with her about being an intern and not a CIA agent,' said Jessica. 'But what about Lucy Donaldson? We now know she went to the Americans for Palestine meeting. Surveillance followed the three of them there.'

'Maybe Lucy is being radicalised by Shehadeh to the Palestinian cause,' said Bec.

'I'm not sure,' said Musa. 'She's a young woman, and Shehadeh is good looking and interesting. I wonder if she might just be falling for him.'

'Yes, and that's the beginning of radicalisation,' Bec responded quickly. 'She's the daughter of a senator. It would be a great win for the Palestinian cause if he could get her over to their side.'

'Yes, that's true,' said Musa.

Bec was pleased that Musa accepted her argument.

Their conversation was interrupted by Jessica's vibrating cell phone rattling upside down on the table. She picked it up and listened for a few minutes, saying little, then put it down.

'You're not going to believe this,' she said. 'The owner of the recycling depot at West Milford has been shot and another garbage truck has been stolen.'

'You're joking. Is he okay?'

'Shot in the head. A woman bringing in a trunkful of recycling found him in his office. I want you over there straight away. West Milford Police are already at the depot, and they called for backup from NYPD. I'm getting our crime scene investigators from Quantico to assist.'

'Can we get DEP Police to fly us down in their fancy helicopter?' said Bec with a grin. 'Assistant Commissioner

Anderson said he would help whenever he could. It would be quicker.'

Jessica grinned back to her former partner. 'Why not? I'll get onto the assistant commissioner and see what I can do. But why go back to the same recycling depot to steal another garbage truck? Why shoot …'

'Joe Jackson,' said Bec.

'That's him, Old Joe. Why not take the truck at night? Why kill the owner during daylight?'

'He had his place alarmed,' said Bec.

'Perhaps our bomber is starting to like killing people,' said Musa quietly with a straight face.

Bec and Jessica looked and stared at Musa. Bec remembered the lesson Musa gave her when they returned to Kensico Dam to look at the site of the bombing. The bomber didn't want to flood low lying districts. The explosion was to make a statement, probably about the situation in Palestine. Now, the second truck had been taken.

'Musa may be right,' she said. 'But one thing is certain. There's going to be another bombing.'

'I damn well hope not,' said Jessica. 'The media will go crazy when they hear another garbage truck has been taken from the same location.'

46

The DEP Police helicopter settled on the grass alongside the runway at Greenwood Lake Airport.

'Thanks for the quick response,' said Bec.

'I'll be here as long as you need.'

'That'll be good,' said Bec. She smiled at the young police pilot. Immediately, she thought of the officer who was shot at Kensico Reservoir.

The two agents walked for less than ten minutes to reach the recycling depot. Bec observed that the local police chief knew what she was doing. The entrance to the depot was blocked with crime scene tape and patrol vehicles were stopping any vehicles entering the road. The West Milford Police command vehicle was parked nearby. They walked straight to it and introduced themselves to Police Chief Tammy Crawford. Another officer was sitting in the vehicle. He entered their arrival time and names into a laptop log of events.

'Good to see you guys,' said the police chief. 'Two garbage trucks from the one depot. That's too much of a coincidence, so we need all the help we can get.'

Bec noted that she seemed calm and appeared to have things well under control.

'The crime scene has been sealed off. The people who've been inside are the woman who found old Joe, Officer Jacobs who responded to the call – he's now doing the log – myself and Detective Hills.'

Bec looked over to Officer Jacobs and nodded.

'We've blocked off each end of the road. No one comes in without my approval.'

'What did you see inside?' asked Musa.

'Not much. Old Joe has owned the depot for years. He was here long before I came to West Milford. The theft of the first truck shook him up, but he kept working, same as always. Anyway, he was lying on his back behind the counter with a bullet hole in his forehead. Bits of his brains and skull were splattered on the wall, so he was probably shot standing up. We couldn't see any bullet casing, but we only had a quick look. It looks like a footprint in the blood underneath the box where the truck keys were kept.'

'Was the truck taken from around the back?' said Musa.

'Don't know.' The police chief sighed. 'I'm assuming that it was parked in the normal spot. After we saw Joe, we backed out and sealed the area.'

'Could the truck be out on a job and not stolen?' questioned Bec.

'It's possible. But the footprint in the blood near the key box makes me think that the truck keys were taken at the time of the shooting. Anyway, after the theft of the first truck and then the bombing, I wasn't taking any chances. That's why I initiated the all-points bulletin and called NYPD.'

Bec and Musa waited at the Command Vehicle as Crime Scene from NYPD arrived. An hour later, Crime

Scene from Quantico landed at Greenwood Lake Airport in one of their FBI helicopters. They guided them to the scene, helping to carry equipment, and then Bec spoke with Tammy Crawford.

'My boss has spoken with NYPD,' said Bec. 'It's been agreed that the FBI will take the lead looking at the crime scene. NYPD will support our guys.'

'Thanks for letting me know. I'm just pleased everyone is here. It helps.'

Two hours later, Bec and Musa watched as old Joe was wheeled from his workplace and placed in the back of the mortuary van. His body would be driven to the Office of the Chief Medical Examiner on East 26th Street, where forensic pathologists were waiting to perform an autopsy.

'Poor bastard,' said Musa, as old Joe was driven from the yard.

47

Paul Shehadeh was angry and frustrated. His efforts to speak to Senator Donaldson had hit a brick wall. His contacts back home knew she was a champion of the two-state solution for Palestine and was a member of the powerful Senate Committee on Foreign Relations. He'd pinned all his hopes on meeting her. But Professor Marshall no longer trusted him and would never introduce him to her. And now his efforts to access the senator through Lucy had failed after he stupidly said that Americans are naïve. His father would be shaking his head with disappointment if he found out the words he used.

'Hello' he said into his vibrating cell phone.

'Hello Nasir.'

Only one person in America called him Nasir.

'Hello Hongwen.'

'Nasir, it is time we had a meeting. Come to the embassy. We need to talk.'

'What about?'

'I'll tell you tomorrow. Be there at ten o'clock.'

Hongwen ended the call before Shehadeh could respond.

48

Shehadeh left his university apartment at 8.30 am and set off for the Hudson River Greenway, four blocks away. The walk, which he knew would take about one and a half hours at a leisurely pace, would allow him to clear his mind.

As planned, he arrived at the large L-shaped building facing the East River five minutes early. Shehadeh thought the upper levels of the Chinese Consulate General were attractive enough, with the green glass of the windows softening the surrounding grey concrete, but the windowless concrete walls of the lower levels were harsh even in a city like New York.

Shehadeh entered the public entrance at 520 12th Avenue. The foyer was large and functional, with rows of metal benches that had fixed grey cushions indicating individual sitting places. He joined a queue of eight people, all Chinese, and waited to slowly shuffle forward. When he reached the front, he stood in place until he was waved forward by the official behind the counter. Again, he stood and waited. Finally, the man behind the glass looked up and spoke.

'Míngchēng?

'Dr Nasir Shehadeh.'

'How can we help you?' the official continued, in perfect English.

'I'm here to see Hua Hongwen.'

The official looked at Shehadeh.

'Please take a seat.'

Five minutes later, the doors of one of the three elevators opened. Hua Hongwen exited in a smart suit and white shirt without a tie. Shehadeh didn't know his formal title, but he was aware he was a relatively senior member of the communist party, even though he was only about forty years of age. Another, older, well-dressed official with groomed hair accompanied him.

'Ni hao, Nasir'

'I'm good, thank you.'

'Let's go where we can talk.'

Hongwen guided Shehadeh to a small room without windows that was accessed from the foyer. The room was sparse, with a bench seat against one wall, which was fronted by a plain wooden table and two chairs. Paul sat on the bench and noticed that Hongwen allowed the older Chinese man to sit first.

'Nasir, how is your research progressing?' asked Hongwen.

'Fine, thank you. I finished comparing the membranes developed by the University of Science and Technology with the French and Italian ones. Of course, the Chinese membranes will be used in the desalination tubes, but the university will be interested in my findings.'

'Of course.'

Hongwen looked hard into his eyes before continuing.

'Nasir, it is time you returned home. It is time to start the project.'

'But I haven't finished my work at Columbia,' Shehadeh said, carefully.

'The work needs to start. You know our engineers can assist you.'

'I need to finish my research. The Americans have the best tunnelling techniques. We'll need to use some of these techniques.'

'You know our tunnelling techniques are just as good. We can help you with them.'

The older Chinese official slowly took a Camel cigarette from a packet and lit it. Shehadeh assessed him as a senior official in the consulate.

'People are asking about you,' said Hongwen. 'The Americans are making enquiries.'

'Why? They already know about me.'

'Then, why are they asking questions?'

Paul had expected something like this and had spent the previous night preparing his response. 'They didn't realise the desalination plant would be built at Arish. I think they don't want the People's Republic of China to get any publicity for helping people in the Middle East.'

'You are a suspect for a bombing,' said Hongwen, suddenly changing tack.

'Bombing! What bombing?'

'The one at Kensico Reservoir.'

'Not true!' said Shehadeh. 'How do you know this?'

Hongwen kept a straight face. 'It is not a matter of how I know this. It is a matter of what is being said.'

Paul Shehadeh's mouth opened but no words came. He

could feel his heart thumping in his chest, and his mind was racing.

'This is ridiculous,' he finally said. 'I had nothing to do with the bombing.'

'You went there with Lucy Donaldson, the senator's daughter.'

'We went there ... Yes. I gave my class an assignment to study water systems that may be relevant to the Middle East.'

Hongwen remained expressionless but changed tack again. 'It was a mistake to come to America. You were advised against it.'

'My enemies are saying these things. It's not true.'

'You are to return home without delay.'

Paul Shehadeh fought for control of the meeting. 'I should finish my research. It would look bad if I walked out of Columbia University.'

The older Chinese expelled smoke and spoke for the first time. His English was perfect.

'Dr Shehadeh, if you want any funding for your project, you will return home at once. This, as they say, is not negotiable. You need to return to your family. They need you.'

Shehadeh studied the man's face. Immediately, he understood the implied threat to his family. He looked at Hongwen, who remained expressionless. Paul could see no sympathy in his eyes.

'I'll be gone in a week.'

'Thank you, Nasir,' said Hongwen. 'Please let me know your flight details.'

Paul Shehadeh left the embassy and hailed the first cab he saw to take him back to Columbia University. After being dropped off on Amsterdam Avenue, he ran into the engineering faculty and down the corridor to Professor Marshall's door. He banged on the door loudly. John Marshall opened it.

'Paul, what's all this banging?'

'Professor, I need to speak to you. I need help.'

'What's wrong?'

'My contact at the Chinese Embassy has asked me to return to Palestine. They want me to start my project straight away.'

'Why?'

Shehadeh hesitated. 'They don't want me to spend any more time in America. I don't think they want America to get any credit for my Living Water project.'

'I see.'

'Professor, can you help me? I need to speak with Senator Donaldson.'

'Why do you need to speak with my wife?'

'I want to offer America my help.'

'What sort of help?'

Shehadeh paused, thinking before saying, 'It's best I speak with the senator.'

'I'm sorry Paul. It's not appropriate for me to speak with her about such matters. Why don't you ring her office?'

Shehadeh shook his head. 'Don't you realise what's happening to America? Don't you realise that China is … What do you say? China is eating your lunch.'

'Oh?'

'America is dying. Look at the buildings in New York. The average age of residential buildings is ninety years. Your water mains are seventy years old. Your sewers are eighty years old. Compare that to Shanghai or a hundred cities in China. Look at the Three Gorges Dam. It dwarfs your famous Hoover Dam. Shanghai and Singapore will replace New York and London as financial capitals.'

As he spluttered on, Paul knew, deep down, he was being crude. But he had to keep going. He had to convince John Marshall. The senator was his only hope.

'Don't you see? My desalination project is a diversion. It takes the world's eyes away from their real goal. Their base at Arish is the final piece in the puzzle. They want to control the trade routes to Europe. New York will die if China dominates world trade.'

John Marshall pursed his lips but didn't say anything. They stared at one another. Finally, he said. 'I'm sorry Paul. I can't help you.'

Shehadeh glared.

'Okay, I'll ring her office,' he said forcefully.

He marched from the room and walked out of the staff building. He pulled his smartphone from his pocket and googled the senator's office. He touched the telephone number that appeared on the screen and waited until the call was answered. When Paul refused to reveal the reason for requesting an appointment, the man who took his call was blunt.

'I will let the senator know you rang,' he said.

Next, he rang Lucy. When she didn't answer his call, he sent her a text. He had been stupid saying Americans were naïve. His father always advised him to control his anger. Now, he'd ruined any chance of helping his people.

Paul started walking dejectedly back to his office. He'd only taken a few steps when his phone rang. He looked at the screen. Lucy was calling.

Words spewed from his mouth.

'What do you mean, you're going home?'

Paul tried to control his fear. 'The Chinese consulate rang and asked me to come in. They want me to return home to start Living Water.'

'When are you leaving?'

'I have to leave next week.'

'That soon? Why?'

'Can we meet? I need to talk.'

'I was just heading to class.'

'Lucy, I'm scared. I can't speak on this phone. Can we meet in the library?'

There was no more hesitation.

'See you in ten minutes.'

Paul was sitting slumped in a chair on the second level when Lucy found him.

'Paul, what's going on?'

'The Chinese want me to go home and start my project.'

'Yes, but what about your research? Your class?'

'I know. It's all happening so quickly. I've spoken to your stepfather; he won't help. Lucy, I need to speak to your mother. Can you help me?'

'Why won't he help?'

'He said it was not appropriate. He won't arrange a meeting.'

Paul reached out and held Lucy's hand. 'Please, speak to your mother. Tell her I want to help America.'

49

When he knocked on the front door of a row houses in Murray Hill, not too far from the United Nations building, Paul Shehadeh had not slept for twenty-four hours. He had received a text message about a meeting with the Senator two hours earlier. He just hoped it meant he would get a fair hearing.

A big man dressed in a dark suit answered the door.

'I've come to speak with the senator.'

The man looked at Shehadeh but didn't ask his name.

'Come in.'

Paul entered the brownstone home.

'Turn around,' the man said as soon as he'd closed the front door. He quickly frisked Shehadeh.

'This way.'

They entered the living room. Senator Donaldson was seated in a lounge chair. Standing beside her was a man of Hispanic appearance.

'Paul, please sit down.'

'Thank you, senator.'

'You wish to speak with me.'

Shehadeh pushed his hand through his hair. 'You know why I'm in America?'

'I know you're a research fellow and a guest lecturer at Columbia University.'

'I came to America to promote my project. Two million people live in Gaza. Nearly three million live in the West Bank. I want to get clean water to my people. The United Nations says water is undrinkable in Gaza. Only four per cent meets World Health Organization guidelines.'

'Yes, I know that. And the Chinese are helping you with your project.'

'Yes, but I don't trust the Chinese to finish it. I fear they are using my project as an excuse to build a base in the Sinai.'

'Why did you approach my husband to supervise you?'

'He is a well-known engineer.'

'And married to me?' said the senator, with a straight face.

Shehadeh paused 'And married to you. Important people in Palestine thought you would support us; you would support us if the Chinese backed out of my Living Water project.'

'Why would they back out of the project?'

'They don't care about the Palestinian people. They want to secure their trade route through the Suez Canal. The desalination plant will be built in Egypt for Egyptians. Unless it suits their needs, they will not build the pipeline to Gaza, let alone to the West Bank.'

'Why should we trust you? You lied in your application to Columbia.'

Shehadeh took a deep breath to steady the nausea he was feeling. He tried to speak calmly. 'I didn't lie in my application. I'm here to get drinking water to my people.'

'I understand that you are married.'

Shehadeh looked quickly at the senator. He expected the question.

'Yes, my wife and two children are in Palestine.'

'You played up to my daughter.'

'I did not deceive Lucy. Your daughter is someone I admire very much. She is intelligent and will be successful in whatever she does.'

The senator did not respond to his comment, so Shehadeh continued.

'Senator, you have an Irish background. You've seen the troubles in Ireland. Your people were displaced by the British. The same thing is happening in the West Bank. My grandfather fought the Jewish settlers when they took his land after the First World War. My father took a different approach. He became a teacher. He wanted to help his people through education. Like his father, his home in Jerusalem was taken, but he did not fight back. He wanted me to get an education, so I could help my people.'

Senator Donaldson gently nodded, and her expression seemed to soften.

'You know Israel is slowly taking everything from us: our homes, our land. Currently, the Palestinian Water Authority must truck water from Israel. And you know what happened?'

'Go on.'

'Now, the water authority is in debt to the Israelis.'

'Yes, I know.'

'After what was done to Jewish people before and during the Second World War, you would think they'd know what it's like to be dispossessed. I'm trying my father's way.

He convinced me to get an education and work with people to improve things: persuasion rather than bullets.'

'I see.'

'You know that Palestinians are divided: one ruling party in Gaza and a different one in the West Bank. I want water to join Gaza and the West Bank. Water will improve our lives, and it will help remove the shackles of the Israelis. The first step is clean drinking water.'

Senator Donaldson looked to the ceiling, and then her eyes roamed the room. She did not comment for a long time. Finally, her eyes returned to Shehadeh. The softness that had shown in her face when he was speaking had gone.

'You are very persuasive Dr Shehadeh. Why did you come to see me?'

Paul could see she was all business.

'I'm leaving America next week. The Chinese are starting their new base. Perhaps, I can help America.'

'How could you help America?'

'I can let your government know what is happening and when it is happening.'

'I see.'

Senator Donaldson glanced at her watch.

'I'm afraid I have a Zoom meeting.' She stood up. 'I suggest you stay and speak with Tony Flores. He's from the CIA. I'll leave you to discuss matters.'

She nodded to the man beside her and left the room.

50

Paul sat in his small apartment adding notes to his remaining lesson plans for Middle Eastern Studies. He wanted to leave the lecturer replacing him with as much information as possible. He reflected on his brief time at Columbia. A few students were attacking their assignment with zeal, comparing a water system in the Middle East to one in America. That pleased him. He felt he was letting his students down.

There was a knock on his door. Opening it, he saw Lucy standing there. Paul was surprised to see her after everything that had happened.

'Lucy.'

Hi, can I come in?'

He hesitated.

'You got your meeting with Mum, didn't you?' she said, raising her eyebrows.

Paul stood back to allow her to enter the small room.

'I wanted to see how you are.'

'Not so good. My trip to America has been a complete failure. I feel I've let my country down, and I've let my students down.'

'Look, why don't we go out for a meal? Maybe that

Mediterranean restaurant you found? I want to try another Middle Eastern dish. My buy.'

Paul looked over at his small table near the kitchenette. It was stacked with library books, which he needed to return, and assorted papers. And his kitchen sink was full of dishes.

'Lucy, I don't know. I've got a lot of stuff to tidy up before I fly out.'

'You need a break. Come on. We'll be back in two hours.'

Paul thought for a moment.

'Okay. I need to get away from all my stuff. So, you've forgiven me?'

'No. But you're going home, and I won't see you again.'

Paul didn't know what to make of her words, but he was too tired to think about them for long.

When they entered the Middle Eastern restaurant on Columbus, Paul asked for a booth at the rear of the diner. Minutes after they were seated, a Chinese couple entered. Paul watched as they were shown to a nearby table. He saw Lucy looking at him and did his best to smile at her. There was no point worrying about the couple or saying anything. Lucy already thought he was overly suspicious. If she only knew.

Paul took a deep breath. 'Shall we order?'

'What's a mezze?'

'Have you tried tapas?'

'Yes, it was lovely.'

'A mezze is similar. You can have one as an appetiser or mains.'

'Let's share a mezze,' said Lucy.

Lucy picked up the wine menu. 'There's a Château Musar from the Bekaa Valley in Lebanon.'

'Bekaa Valley. I hear some of their wines are nice.'

'Do you drink alcohol? I never thought of asking.'

'Lots of young Muslims drink alcohol. The Chinese introduced me to beer and a friend introduced me to Lebanese wines.' Paul smiled. 'Just don't tell my grandfather.'

Their pita bread arrived with small serves of hummus and taramasalata. Kibbeh followed. By the time the lamb dish was served, Paul could tell Lucy was slightly tipsy, and so he made sure to order coffee to go with their baklava.

When they had finished their coffee, Lucy reached across the table and touched his arm.

'Why don't we get out of here?'

She stood up and placed some money on the table. As they left, she put her hand in his. Paul stopped and turned Lucy towards him. Just the sight of her dissolved his sadness.

'You're no longer my lecturer,' she said, moving closer.

Paul leaned away from her and looked into her eyes, trying to assess what was happening.

'What about your mother?'

'Mum's never going to know.'

Paul Shehadeh woke in the early hours of the morning as Lucy was easing herself from his arms. He pretended to be asleep while she dressed, then he opened his eyes and watched as she quietly walked over to the door of the apartment and left. He was glad she had come into his life. His plans hadn't included Lucy Donaldson when he came to America, but he realised that he would not have spoken to Senator Donaldson without her help. Now it was time to move on, to return home and start his project.

51

Lucy quietly closed the door to Paul's apartment and moved down the stairs. She felt a sense of triumph, getting what she wanted. The Mediterranean meal was nice, and the evening back at Paul's apartment was positive – as well as successful. She found him caring and tender.

The cool breeze hit her as she left the building, so she zipped her jacket higher and walked quickly through the quiet streets. She entered the parking garage on W 112nd Street and went over to the lifts. When one arrived, she entered and pressed the button to level four. It rose quickly, the doors opened, and she stepped out onto an almost empty floor.

Lucy walked quickly over to her mother's Mercedes and activated its remote. The lights flashed. She reached to open the driver's door when a strong arm wrapped around her body from behind. Lucy opened her mouth to scream but her cry was muffled as a bag was pulled over her head and held tightly around her neck. She tried to breathe, but the breath drew plastic into her mouth. She grabbed at the bag, trying to get some air. But the strength was draining from her arms. Blackness enveloped her.

Lucy felt a jolt and opened her eyes. She could only see darkness, but slowly her eyes adjusted to the small amount of light filtering into the small space. From the sound of the exhaust growling in her ears, she could tell she was in the trunk of a car.

The plastic bag was gone, but there was tape across her mouth. She tried to move, but her hands and feet were bound. All she could do was touch the end of one of the plastic ties around her wrists with her middle finger.

There was another jolt from a dip in the road, and soon after the car sped up, as if it had moved onto a highway. Lucy guessed they had been travelling for thirty minutes when the vehicle stopped, waited and then drove forward and stopped again. The car door slammed shut, and then there was a sound of a shed door closing. A few seconds later, the trunk opened.

'Hello, Lucy.'

Lucy squinted from the glare of the overhead light and tried to focus on the person hovering over her. Slowly, her eyes adjusted. The student Paul had told to stop texting in class leaned forward and ripped the tape from her face.

'You? What do you want? I've done nothing to you. Let me go.'

'I'll let you go, but first I want the password to your phone.'

'What if I don't give it to you?'

The guy smiled, but the smile had no warmth in it. 'I think you will.'

He reached behind his back and pulled an ornate

dagger and its sheath from his belt. He moved close to her and slowly pulled the dagger from its scabbard, revealing a large, curved blade. The blade moved towards her face. Lucy pulled back in fear until the rear of the trunk stopped her retreat. She felt the point of the blade against her skin and closed her eyes as it cut into her cheek. She screamed and blood from the cut ran down her face and into her mouth.

'A few cuts across your pretty cheeks should do the job. If not, I'll cut out an eye.'

Lucy started to sob. Tears mingled with the blood in her mouth.

'I think you're starting to understand me.'

She felt the blade against her other cheek.

'Another cut? Or the password?'

'Lovergirl,' she blurted out.

'That's better. Are you Shehadeh's lover girl?'

Lucy kept quiet, too frightened to speak. She managed to shake her head.

'What were you doing in his apartment, Lucy?'

She shook her head, again not saying anything, but more tears flowed. She knew any resistance she had was fading.

He pulled up her top and used it to wipe away the tears and blood from her face then ripped a length of tape from its roll.

'Now, the tape will stay in place. No noise from you, Lucy, otherwise more blood will flow.'

He smiled and shut the trunk, and again she was in darkness.

52

The largest of the five incident rooms in the FBI's New York headquarters was dedicated to the Kensico Dam bombing. Exhibits, files and flowcharts had surged in number throughout the investigation and were competing for space.

The remains of the truck and Officer Lehman's patrol vehicle were in an Upstate storage facility, laid out in a similar way aircraft accident investigators lay out the pieces recovered from aircraft crashes. As much as possible, parts had been placed in positions relative to how the truck and patrol vehicle existed prior to the explosion. The remnants of the cabin of the garbage truck sat in front of the ruins of the compactor and the front wheels. The battered remains of the patrol vehicle were placed at the rear of the truck. It was positioned the same distance away from the garbage truck as it was at Kensico Reservoir.

Smaller exhibits from the bombing were still held in the exhibit room downstairs. Jessica White needed more space, and boxes had to be moved to their Upstate storage. Bec heard Musa mutter something about mundane work forced on investigators.

Bec found a list compiled by Crime Scene that she had

not seen previously. It was a list of items that were found within 100 metres of the blast. Crime scene examiners had bagged and marked each item, and they had used GPS co-ordinates on a digital map to record the exact location where the items were found. She read through the list. It comprised five disposable coffee cups found in a variety of locations, an empty cigarette packet, one hundred and seventy-nine discarded cigarette butts, a pair of broken sunglasses, a baseball cap and a used condom. There was nothing much out of the ordinary.

'Wait a minute.' Bec said out loud as she rushed for the door.

'Where are you going?' Musa called out.

'Tell you when I get back.'

Bec ran down the stairwell to the locked storeroom two levels below. After signing in, she found the four large exhibit boxes she needed. She discovered what she was looking for in the second box: a baseball cap with 'Columbia' embroidered on it.

'Come to Mumma,' Bec said. She left the storeroom and bolted up the fire stairs, taking three steps at a time.

'We may have the right guy after all,' she said, bursting into the incident room.

'Why? What have you got?'

'A Columbia University baseball cap was found at the scene,' she said, showing Musa the exhibit.

Both agents stared into the paper bag without touching the cap.

'Where was it found?'

'The crime scene map shows it was found in the tree line on the driver's side of the truck.'

Musa looked at the map. 'Shehadeh was wearing a base-ball cap at Kensico Reservoir before the bombing.'

'Exactly,' she said, excitedly. 'I wonder if we can see the words on the cap in the video.'

She started looking for the computer folder holding the CCTV file and found it after a quick search. The two agents looked at the video and enlarged photographs of Paul Shehadeh and Lucy Donaldson acting like tourists at the reservoir. The cap was similar in colour, and there was a word embroidered on it. It looked like 'Columbia', but they couldn't be certain.

'So maybe we do have a suspect worth looking at,' said Bec. 'I'll brief Jessica. Take the cap to the lab and ask them to have a look at it for DNA and anything else they can find. On the way back, call into the computer lab and see if they can enhance the pictures.'

'I'm going. I'll push things to give it priority.'

Bec went to Jessica White's office to brief her about the cap. She was still there when Musa returned and joined them.

'Guess what?' said Bec to Musa, excited for the second time in an hour. 'We've got a match with the bullets.'

'Ballistics made the match in four days,' said Jessica 'Fantastic work.'

'Crime Scene found the bullet that killed old Joe in the wall behind the counter. It wasn't found straight away because bits of brain and blood dripped into the bullet hole. The bullet was another nine-millimetre metal jacket slug. Ballistics are confident it's a match to the one found at Kensico Dam.'

'So,' said Jessica White, 'both garbage trucks were taken by the same people.'

'Two trucks, two killings, same gun. Sure looks like it,' said Bec.

'What about the front loader? Where are we with that?'

'Still no luck with the front loader,' said Bec. 'It's just disappeared. We've checked CCTV on the main roads around West Milford … Nothing. We're thinking they either used back roads, or it didn't go far. Could be in a shed somewhere close. Maybe they live in the district.'

'Every television network across the country is showing pictures of a similar truck,' said Jessica. 'We're getting good coverage, as you would expect. We've had over five hundred reports of White-GMC front loaders. Teams around the country and local police are chasing them down.'

'Good,' answered Bec.

'Where was Shehadeh at the time?'

'Forensics estimates old Joe died around ten in the morning,' said Bec. 'Unfortunately, surveillance lost Shehadeh in the university grounds about seven in the morning after he left his apartment. It's a bit hard for some of our surveillance people to blend in with students, but his cell phone location showed that he stayed around the university.'

'So, that lets him off the hook?'

'Unless he left his cell phone in his office,' said Musa. Bec gave him a slight smile and nodded in agreement.

'How long was he missing?'

'About five hours,' said Bec. 'There was enough time to get to West Milford, kill old Joe, take the truck and get back to Manhattan. It would be tight but possible.'

'What else are we getting from surveillance?'

'Not much. He's moving between his apartment and

the university. He's contacted the Chinese Embassy and went there on May 18. CIA believes his contact is Hua Hongwen, a senior political operative. We're asking National Security and CIA if they can tell us anything about him.'

Bec decided it was time to introduce some of Musa's concerns about Shehadeh being a weak suspect.

'There's still a problem with Shehadeh. He needed a vehicle to get to West Milford. We don't think that he's got one. So, he must have rented a vehicle, or someone must have taken him there. We're checking his credit cards to see if he rented anything.'

'What about the senator's daughter? Would she drive him to West Milford?'

'She's close to Shehadeh,' said Bec. 'She seems to have fallen for him. It's possible,'

'I see it as a student crush at this stage,' said Musa.

'True, but Lucy Donaldson is active on social media. She is promoting the Palestinian cause, and her posts are becoming more strident.'

'Okay, said Jessica. 'We know more than one person must be involved. Let's find any contacts of Shehadeh we don't know about. I want surveillance on Lucy Donaldson but keep it tight. I don't want the FBI director getting phone calls from Senator Donaldson late at night.'

'Anyway, we can't leave talking to Shehadeh any longer. The second garbage truck and now the baseball cap. We need to speak to him. At the same time, we can get a sample of his hair. There may be some hair caught in the Velcro on the baseball cap. I couldn't see any, but I didn't want to take it out of the exhibit bag.'

'Don't forget to get a sample of his saliva for DNA, as well,' said Jessica.

'Of course.'

'Where is he now?'

'His cell phone shows he's in his apartment,' said Musa.

Jessica White checked her smart watch and headed for the door. 'I'll have to brief the boss.'

'Okay. I'll organise a warrant to break in, if needed,' said Bec. 'Crime Scene may be able to get hair samples from a comb and DNA from his toothbrush or coffee cup.'

53

Paul Shehadeh walked listlessly around his small apartment, looking for things to do. He'd finished preparing lesson plans for his replacement, and it was too early to start packing for his flight back home.

He bent down and leant on the side of his bed looking for his sneakers. He thought he would get some fresh air and walk to the Hudson River. He found the sneakers hidden behind the suitcase he'd stuffed under the bed when he first arrived. So much, yet so little had happened since then.

He sighed. He was heading home in three days; there was nothing more he could do.

Paul's phone rang as he was heading out for his walk.

'Hello?'

'Paul, it's Rosa. Have you seen Lucy?'

He hesitated, not wanting to admit they were together last night.

'Why are you asking?'

'She's missing.'

'What do you mean?'

'She didn't go home last night. Her mum rang me asking where she was. Wasn't she with you?'

'We went out to dinner. But she went home afterwards.'

'What time did she leave you?'

He hesitated again. 'Sometime after midnight. Have you tried her phone?'

'Yes, it keeps going to messages. Did she say what she was doing today?'

'No, I thought she'd be at the university. She had an assignment to finish. I'll check the library and study room.'

'Ring me back.'

'Yes,' he replied, running his hand through his hair. 'Yes, I will.'

Shehadeh left the apartment and walked quickly to the university, his mind racing. He had no idea what could have happened to Lucy, but he was the last person to see her. If he couldn't find her, he'd be answering some awkward questions.

After an hour, he headed back to his apartment building. Within a couple of minutes, his phone rang.

'Any luck?' Rosa asked.

'I checked everywhere. Lucy's not at the university.'

While he was talking, Paul continued to walk towards his apartment. He saw a large white van parked out front. There was constant movement of people in and out of the entrance. Moving closer, he could see they were all dressed in white protective coveralls that continued up their necks and covered their heads. On the rear of the vehicle was a sign saying FBI Crime Scene.

He was staring at the van when he heard Rosa ask, 'Where are you, now?'

Paul's mind raced. He said quickly, 'I'll get back to you,' and ended the call. He crossed the road and headed down the nearest alleyway and out of sight.

54

B ec waited with Musa while explosives experts wearing protective clothing checked the apartment door for any trip wires before allowing anyone to enter. The experts then entered the apartment and checked the rooms for any explosives or chemicals to make bombs. None were found. Bec reminded them to check the refrigerator for dichloroacetylene, which needed to be kept cool, even though she was sure they didn't have to be told.

She didn't want anything to go wrong.

After the bomb technicians had ensured the apartment was clear of explosives, Bec was able to enter for a quick look and to give a final briefing to the crime scene team leader. Crime Scene were instructed to search for DNA and fingerprints and seize any evidence that might link Shehadeh to the bombing or the death of Old Joe. Also, they were looking for computer equipment and cell phones, including older cheaper models, which could be used to trigger a detonator. The actions of the team were being videoed, and Bec knew any items that were seized would be photographed where they were found.

Before Bec had finished talking to the crime scene team leader, the explosives experts entered the apartment for the second time. They had returned to the FBI van to remove their heavy, protective clothing and replace it with the white coveralls used by crime scene personnel. This time they had sensitive equipment with them to test shoes and clothing for traces of ammonium nitrate and other chemicals used in explosives.

Crime Scene found strands of black hair on a brush in the bathroom and two dirty coffee cups in the kitchen space. Lipstick was on the rim of one of the cups. The brush and coffee cups were seized for DNA evidence and placed in marked paper bags. Shoes were found in the bedroom. Bec didn't think the pattern on the sole of the shoe matched the bloody footprint at old Joe's office, but the shoes would be checked to see if their size matched the footprint.

When Shehadeh didn't return to his apartment, the two agents went to Columbia University and asked security to open his office for them. They had hoped to find his laptop, but the search revealed nothing. They returned to the apartment to discuss their next possible moves to find Shehadeh. Jessica White was waiting with a worried look on her face.

'How's it going? I'm getting a lot of heat from the boss.'

'Shehadeh has disappeared,' said Bec. 'He didn't return to his apartment, and his phone is switched off, so we can't track him.'

'It's not just Shehadeh,' said Jessica. 'Lucy Donaldson has gone missing.'

'You're joking?' said Bec.

'No joke.'

'When did she go missing?'

'Last night. Shehadeh and Donaldson had a meal together, and she didn't go home after. She was driving her mother's vehicle. We found it in a parking lot near Shehadeh's apartment. Her cell phone has been turned off as well.'

'They're together?'

'Looks like it.' She paused. 'That's not all. Her mother is talking to our Director in Washington, who's asking what's going on.'

Musa raised his eyebrows and gave an extended whistle.

'The Director is asking why we didn't pull Shehadeh in earlier. He's saying it should have been done as soon as the second garbage truck was stolen. Shehadeh and Donaldson must be found. The boss is even talking about bringing agents back from holidays.'

Bec looked at Musa and shook her head. There was no need to speak. They knew the pressure on all of them was going to be intense.

55

Shehadeh caught the subway to move as far away as possible from his apartment in a relatively short period of time. He assumed his calls and location were being monitored, so he switched his phone off. He got off one train and moved to another. At the end of the second trip, he turned his phone on and rang Tony Flores at the CIA but only got his messaging service. He switched his phone off again and jumped on another subway train and exited at Bowling Green in the financial district. He walked to Battery Park Esplanade and decided to switch on his phone. A text message from Flores appeared: 'Go to FBI HQ and ask for agents Bekele or Halmat'.

He turned off his cell phone again, wondering what the point of a contact in the CIA was, if that was all he could do. He headed back to the subway to get a train travelling towards Central Park. He wanted wide open spaces between him and any other person. In the train, he considered all his options. There weren't many.

He walked Central Park, deciding he had to trust Tony Flores and would contact Halmat. With a name like that, there was a chance the agent was Muslim. Shehadeh stopped and switched on his phone. He took a deep breath and called FBI headquarters.

'Halmat.'

It was a man's voice, a bit abrupt.

'I understand you're looking for me.'

'Who's calling?'

'Paul Shehadeh.'

'Paul, where are you?

'Never mind that. What's your first name, Agent Halmat?'

'Why do you ask?

'I want to know if you're a Muslim.'

There was a pause. 'Musa.'

'So, you are a Muslim?'

'Why do you want to know?'

'I'm going to hang up if you don't answer my question. Are you a Muslim?'

'Yes, Paul. I'm a Muslim. Why do you want to know?'

'I want to talk to someone who might understand me.'

'Where are you?'

'Never mind, I'm sure you'll trace my location soon. Where were you born, Musa?'

'I was born in New York. My father and mother were Kurds.'

'So, you understand what it is to be a minority, just like Palestinians.'

'Paul, we need to speak with you.'

'Agent Halmat, I did not blow up the truck at Kensico Reservoir. I'm being set up. You must believe me.'

'Come in, and we can talk about it. Where are you?'

'Central Park but I will be gone by the time you get here. Believe me, I'm being set up. I want the support of the

Americans for my project. I don't want to hurt Americans.'

'Paul, I understand what it's like to be a minority. I want to help you, but you must come in.'

'Who doesn't want my project to go ahead, Agent Halmat? You think about that.'

'Paul—'

Shehadeh ended the call and joined the crowds on Fifth Avenue. He moved towards Times Square at a pace that was faster than other pedestrians, regularly checking both sides of the street for anyone travelling at the same speed. He needed time to think. When he saw the AMC cinema on 42nd Street, he went inside and bought a ticket to an Aamir Khan movie then sat in the theatre wondering what to do.

After fifteen minutes, he decided to ring Tony Flores again to ask him to be present at any interview with Bekele and Halmat. He switched on his smart phone. It dinged and his screen indicated he had a message.

56

The message was from Lucy. 'Can you meet me at the golf course at Van Cortlandt Park? It's important.' Paul's thumbs raced across the electronic keyboard. 'Are you alright?' There was no reply, so he rang her number. 'Please leave a message' was all he heard. He left a voice message and waited for Lucy to respond. After ten minutes, he walked quickly to Broadway and jumped on the Line 1 train.

The sun was low in the sky when Paul exited Van Cortlandt Park station on 242nd Street and walked toward the golf course. Ten minutes later, he arrived at the parking lot. It was empty except for a black BMW sedan. Lucy was nowhere to be seen. He reached for his phone and rang Lucy's number. Once again, all he got was 'Please leave a message'.

Paul walked over to the vehicle and looked inside. Empty. He looked around the parking lot again and called out.

'Lucy!'

A pair of birds flew from a nearby tree, startling him. Then, he heard a loud thump coming from the trunk of the BMW. He knocked on the lid.

'Lucy!'

There was another bang and a muffled cry.

'Hang on, Lucy.'

The trunk was locked, so Paul went to the driver's door to try and access the trunk release. He had his hand on the doorhandle when he heard movement. He turned to see what was causing the sound. Something struck his temple and the evening sky turned black.

57

Bec was back at the office working overtime with Musa. Shehadeh had disappeared, and they were looking for leads that might indicate his location. The triangulation of his last known cell phone signals indicated he was at Van Cortland Park sixty three minutes after being near Times Square. Then, his phone was switched off and he was gone. Bec was checking the most recent calls Paul Shehadeh had made from his smart phone, while Musa was checking the list of emails compiled by intelligence operatives.

'Bec, come and look at this. Shehadeh contacted Industrial Chemical Supplies on the day he arrived in America.'

'What? Why didn't we find that earlier?' She moved over to him and looked at the list of emails.

'Intelligence started checking emails on the day of the bombing and worked backwards. They had four months of emails to check.'

Bec's phone rang, interrupting them.

'Bekele.'

'Come to my office,' said Jessica. 'Intelligence may have something.'

They climbed the fire stairs to the next level. Bec knocked and they both entered.

'Do you know Cassie?' Jessica asked, looking at her computer screen. Cassie Spargo, FBI Analyst, was peering over her left shoulder, also looking at the screen.

Bec smiled at Cassie. 'Yes, we've worked together before. Heroin smuggling from Lebanon through Cyprus.'

'Now, I remember,' said Jessica. 'Cassie's collating all the CCTV vision that was found from door knocking the homes and businesses around Kensico Dam and on the roads leading to the reservoir. She's found something interesting. Come around and have a look at the screen.'

Jessica stood up. 'Cassie, grab my seat. Back up the vision and tell them what you've got.'

Jessica White moved around and stood behind Bec.

Cassie Spargo clicked 'play'. 'We got the vision from Valhalla Railway Station. There are six cameras. I checked the vision an hour before and an hour after the bombing, but I missed it. I didn't pick it until I went through the vision again: all the vision for one month prior to the bombing and two days afterwards. It's been long and slow.'

'Missed what? asked Bec.

'Let's see if you can spot it,' said Jessica White, as the analyst fast forwarded the vision to the morning of the bombing.

'This vision is from the camera covering the parking lot,' said Cassie. 'It's a long-distance shot, and I've enhanced it as much as possible.'

The time clock on the vision showed cars arriving at the parking lot for the early commute to Manhattan. Cassie stopped fast forwarding the vision at five minutes prior to the bombing and pressed 'stop' five minutes after the bombing.

'I could play more, but it's the same. Did you pick it?'

'A vehicle or something else?' asked Musa.

'A vehicle,' said Cassie.

'What time did the first morning train leave?' asked Bec.

'Fifteen minutes after the bombing.'

'And what time did the first train arrive at the station?'

'An hour after the bombing.'

'Play five minutes before and after the bombing again.' said Bec.

Bec pointed. 'There, when the video's clock was showing two minutes after the bombing. 'The black SUV leaving the parking lot.'

Bec saw Cassie Spargo smile and was pleased she'd spotted it before Musa.

'You've got it.'

'It's the only vehicle leaving the parking lot,' said Jessica. 'Everyone else is arriving to catch the train. Why would someone leave a railway station parking lot early in the morning when the first train doesn't arrive for another hour?'

'What about the licence plate? Could you make it out?' Bec asked.

'Unfortunately, no. I tried enhancing the picture in a number of ways, but we can't bring it up enough.'

'What's the make?'

'An older model BMW X7 SUV.'

'Isn't that the same as one of the vehicles at Industrial Chemical Supplies?' said Bec.

'The fancy Lexus, an expensive BMW sedan and an older black BMW SUV were parked by the office,' said Musa. 'That could be the BMW SUV.'

'Well, it's time to revisit Industrial Chemical Supplies,'

said Bec. 'We've found one of Shehadeh's helpers in America. John Tomlin was contacted by Shehadeh the day he arrived in America, and he just happens to supply chemicals that can be used in explosives.'

'Any vision shows the driver?' asked Musa.

'Only from the rear of the vehicle. We think there were two or three people in it.'

'Could any of the people in the BMW be a woman?' Bec asked, wondering if Lucy Donaldson had helped him with the bombing.

'Can't tell.'

58

An hour before sun-up, Musa parked their unmarked vehicle at the rear of the Port Jervis Police building. Within five minutes, a second unmarked car and a plain white Ford Transit van pulled in beside them. The Chief of Police and two officers were waiting inside for them. Bec briefed them on the plan for the operation, which was for the two plain vehicles to arrive at Industrial Chemical Supplies at eight in the morning when the office opened. The Transit van carrying Crime Scene and an explosives expert would arrive half an hour later. Local police would remain at the station to support the FBI, if needed.

A young officer from Port Jervis told them he often walked past the warehouse with his dog at around 7.00 am and would say hello to the storeman as he was opening the warehouse. So, the plan was moved forward an hour.

Five minutes before seven, the two unmarked cars left the Port Jervis Police building and travelled to the industrial estate. Agent Lucas Smythe and his partner, Graham

Jacobs, positioned their vehicle down the road from the entrance to the warehouse to provide support, if it was needed. Musa continued and drove into the parking lot just as a young man in high vis clothing was unlocking the warehouse door.

'Musa, go to the storeman and hold him,' said Bec, as she opened the car door. 'I'll check the office.'

Bec went straight to the office and banged on the locked front door. There was no answer, so she moved to the warehouse.

'What's your name?' she asked the young black American.

'Bobby.'

'Your full name.'

'Robert James Brown. Everyone calls me Bobby.'

'You work here?'

'Yeh, I work in the warehouse. What do you want?'

'FBI. We're making enquiries about explosives used in the Kensico Dam bombing.'

'I know. You came here before.'

'That's right. You were in the office when we arrived.'

'What time does Mr Tomlin get to work?'

'He doesn't. He's dead.'

Bec was taken by surprise. 'What happened?' she asked. 'When did he die?'

'About four weeks ago. JJ said he had a heart attack.'

'JJ?'

'His son.'

'Who's running the place now?' she asked.

'JJ.'

'And where's he now?

Bobby Brown shook his head. 'Don't know.'

Musa stepped closer to Brown and looked down at him. 'What do you mean, you don't know?' The storeman wilted. 'I don't know. He's the boss now. His father was always on time, eight o'clock on the dot. JJ arrives when he feels like it.'

'What's in the warehouse?' Bec asked

'ACTi zyme, caustic soda, ferric sulphate and hydrogen peroxide are the main ones.'

'You know your chemicals.'

Bobby Brown relaxed a little with Bec's softer approach.

'Mr Tomlin sent me on some training courses. He was okay.'

Bec's two-way radio squelched. As she answered, she was watching Bobby Brown stare out at the road.

'Bec, you by yourself?' asked Agent Smythe.

Bec moved out of Brown's hearing.

'Go ahead.'

'A black BMW SUV drove past slowly and then took off.'

Bec moved back to the storeman and eyed Bobby Brown. 'You were looking at the street. Who was driving the black BMW SUV that just drove by?'

Bobby Brown swallowed. 'It was JJ's vehicle. He'd be driving it.'

'Get after it,' said Bec over the two-way. She watched as their support vehicle sped past. 'Musa can you have a look for the vehicle, as well? Just in case.'

Musa left rubber on the surface of the parking lot as he sped towards the main street of Port Jervis. Crime Scene arrived a few moments later and unlocked the front door of the office complex within thirty seconds of getting the lock picking set from their van.

Bec returned to Bobby Brown. 'Now, Mr Brown, you and I are going to have a little talk. I want to know why your boss didn't want to come to work today. Come with me.'

She took Brown into John Tomlin's office and pointed to one of two visitors' chairs.

'Sit down.'

Bec sat on the edge of the desk looking down at the storeman.

'How long have you worked here, Bobby?'

'Three months.'

'You said you work in the warehouse?'

'Yeh, I'm the storeman.'

'You're a storeman who knows chemicals. How did you get the job?'

Brown hesitated.

'I'll ask one more time,' she said, hardening her tone. 'How did you get the job?'

'I knew JJ from our time in the infantry. We were in the same unit in Afghanistan.'

'So, you know JJ well. Why did he drive past and not come to work?'

'I don't know. He doesn't tell me anything. Just what to do.'

Bec saw Musa pulling up outside the building.

'You just sit there and think about things,' she said to Brown. 'When I come back, you better start telling me what you do know.'

She left the office to speak with Musa.

'Lost him,' he said, raising his voice to be heard over a siren that was blaring in the background. 'The boys are still looking. I called into the police station and told them what happened. They're searching as well.'

'Let's hope they find him.'

'How did you go with the storeman?' asked Musa.

'I've got him in Tomlin's office. He knows more than he's saying. He was a soldier in Afghanistan with the son. He can sit there for a while. Come on.'

Bec and Musa quickly searched the office area, while the crime scene agents were photographing and itemising the contents of the warehouse. Nothing grabbed their attention, but they knew the value would be in the computer files and the safe found in the small storeroom accessed from Tomlin's office. Crime Scene would seize the computers, and the safe would be cut open if the digital combination could not be found.

'I think it's time we had another quiet word with Bobby Brown.'

They were heading to John Tomlin's office when the agents from their support vehicle caught up with them.

'We've found the BMW,' said Smythe.

'Where?' asked Bec.

'Outside of town,' said Jacobs. 'Burnt out on a back road.'

'What about JJ? The storeman thought he lived with his father.'

'The local guys thought the same,' said Smythe. 'We checked his father's place and it's empty. No furniture inside and a for sale sign out front. The neighbours say Tomlin's son hasn't lived there since his father died.'

'Thanks,' said Bec. 'We'll try and get something out of the storeman.'

Bobby Brown was quietly smoking when Bec re-entered John Tomlin's office. Musa followed her in. This time, he sat on the edge of the desk and loomed over Brown. Bec sat in the other visitors' chair and pulled it in close to the storeman.

'Alright Bobby,' she said, 'now's the time to speak up ... before you dig a bigger hole for yourself.'

Brown hesitated. 'I s'pose you want to know about the Arabian dagger Mr Tomlin killed himself with. The one he brought back from the Middle East.'

Bec glanced at Musa. 'How do you know that?'

'I saw JJ swap the knives. Mr Tomlin cut his wrists with a fancy Arabian dagger, but JJ swapped it for a kitchen knife before the cops came. I s'pose he was worried you were here for that.'

'Where were you when you saw JJ swap knives?' she asked.

'I was in the warehouse when JJ came looking for Mr Tomlin. JJ was ... I don't know ... He looked worried. So, I followed him back into the main office. Mr Tomlin's office door was locked, so JJ kicked it in.'

'What happened then?'

'I stayed back. But I heard JJ yelling, and then he came out with the fancy dagger. He didn't see me at first. But when he did, he told me to keep my mouth shut.'

'What about the truck bombing at Kensico Dam?' said Musa. 'What do you know about that?'

Brown licked his lips and shook his head. 'Nothing.'

'Where were you on the morning of Wednesday, twenty-eighth of April?' asked Bec.

'I was home in bed.'

'That was a very quick answer, Bobby.'

Brown didn't respond.

'What about JJ? Was he involved?'

'You'd have to ask him.'

Musa leaned over and poked Brown in the chest. 'Don't be a smart arse, Bobby.'

'You were dishonourably discharged from the military for killing a civilian, weren't you?' said Bec.

Brown shuffled in his chair. 'Yeh.'

'JJ was discharged for the same thing, wasn't he?'

Brown looked at the floor. 'Yeh.'

Bec moved her face closer to Brown. 'Bobby, you should know my Muslim colleague here doesn't like soldiers who served in Afghanistan. And he hates soldiers who kill civilians.'

Bec saw him glance at Musa.

'Now, is there anything else you have to tell us?'

'No, I've told you everything,' he said, looking at the floor.

'Sit there and don't move Bobby, we'll be back later,' and Bec signalled Musa to step outside.

'How did you know Bobby Brown killed a civilian?' asked Musa, when they moved out to the veranda of the office to catch some fresh air and talk about how they were going to find JJ.

'I asked Jessica to do a quick check while you were chasing down the BMW.'

'He knows more than he's saying.'

'Sure does, and Industrial Chemical Supplies is becoming more and more interesting. The manager has committed suicide and his son does a flyer when he sees our vehicles. We need to find Tomlin Jr, and I'd like to know who owns the business.'

59

The doors to one of the many lifts in the Empire State Building closed and Bec pushed the button. The lift ascended quickly to the 72nd floor. She and Musa left the lift and they saw the glass entrance door. The name, Globle Logistics, was etched into the glass. Bec opened the door and moved to the reception desk.

'Agents Bekele and Halmat from the FBI. We're here to see Mr Moses.'

'Is he expecting you?' asked the impeccably dressed receptionist, who displayed a face that would be appropriate at a funeral.

'Yes, he is,' replied Bec maintaining a straight face. Of course, he was expecting them. They'd raided his warehouse the day before.

The receptionist returned a curious look before replying. 'Just a moment.'

She stood and moved to a set of double doors about ten steps from her desk. She knocked, entered and closed the doors behind her. Two minutes later, she opened them.

'This way,' she said.

The two agents entered a large, plush office facing the Hudson River. Bec immediately noticed an elaborately decorated dagger in a secure glass case mounted on a stand. It sat between two chairs near the window. Sunlight moved through the glass and bounced from the largest stone in its handle. Musa stared at it.

'I see you've noticed my prized possession,' said Richard Moses. 'Eighteenth century. The sun at this time of day brings the best out of it. The workmanship is amazing. The blade is Damascus steel but, from the design of the handle, the experts believe it was made in Oman.'

Musa remained staring at the dagger. Bec knew he was thinking about his investigation into stolen artefacts. She opened the conversation. 'Mr Moses, I understand Globle Logistics owns Industrial Chemical Supplies at Port Jervis.'

'That's correct.'

'What does Globle Logistics do?'

'We transport and supply chemicals across the world. Primarily, to water treatment plants.'

'I understand that Globle Logistics is headquartered in Israel?'

'Yes. Tel Aviv.'

'And Industrial Chemical Supplies is part of Globle Logistics?'

'I run Globle Logistics' operations in America, and Industrial Chemical Supplies is one of my businesses. I understand you visited yesterday.'

'We were making enquiries about chemicals that may have been used in the truck bombing at Kensico Reservoir.'

'I see. A very important investigation. I'm sure everything is in order. We are very careful about that sort of thing.'

'Who manages Industrial Chemical Supplies?'

'John Tomlin managed the warehouse until a short time ago. Unfortunately, he died recently.'

'I understand he committed suicide.'

'Yes, terrible business. He was a good man, and he served his country very well. Ex-CIA, you know.'

'Do you know why he committed suicide?'

'Not really. His son said he was depressed about getting old.'

'His son? John Tomlin Jr?'

'Yes, JJ.'

'Do you know where his son is?'

'He should be at the warehouse.'

'No, he isn't at work.

'That's very unusual.'

'How did you know we visited the warehouse?'

'I rang the warehouse early this morning. The storeman mentioned it.'

'Do you know where JJ lives?'

'I thought he lived with his father.'

'It seems that he moved out at about the time his father died. Do you know where he might be?'

Moses looked out of his window. 'As I said, John Tomlin was a good man. But I know his son had some problems from his time in Afghanistan. John asked if he could work at Industrial Chemical Supplies. Naturally, I said yes.'

'That's very good of you,' said Bec, giving him a soft smile. 'What problems did he have in Afghanistan?'

'He wouldn't tell his father, but I made some enquiries. I understand he was involved in the shooting of a civilian and was dishonourably discharged. Can you tell me what's going on?'

'We would like to speak with him to make sure his chemical inventory is in order. And you don't know where he is?'

'No.'

'Please tell him to contact us when you speak with him. We'll give our details to your receptionist.'

'Certainly.'

Bec turned to leave the office. 'Agent Bekele, I have a property in the woods in New Jersey. It has an airstrip and JJ has a light plane hangered there. You may like to check there.'

'Where in New Jersey?'

'My receptionist will give you the details.'

'Thank you, Mr Moses. Please let us know if he contacts you.'

60

The receptionist provided Bec with the location of the airstrip and home of Richard Moses. It was near Layton, New Jersey, thirty minutes from Port Jervis. Bec thanked her, and the two FBI agents entered the empty elevator and pressed the button for the ground floor.

'You were staring at that dagger for a long time,' said Bec. 'Do you think it was one of the pair of khanjars taken from the museum in Baghdad?'

'I'm sure of it. Tomlin probably killed himself with the other one.'

'I wonder where the other one is?'

'There was only paperwork, credit cards and some money in Tomlin's safe,' said Musa. 'My guess is JJ has it.'

'So, the Tomlins at Industrial Chemical Supplies are Shehadeh's American contacts?'

'It sure looks like it. Shehadeh contacted Tomlin the day he arrived in America. The two garbage trucks were stolen from West Milford in New Jersey, not far from Industrial Chemical Supplies. The explosives were stolen from Sterling Forest State Park, which is only half an hour away. The second truck just disappeared: no sightings at all. I bet it's in a shed not far away. Probably at Moses' property.'

'The second garbage truck is a worry. It's likely they're preparing it for another bombing.'

'We've got to get back to the office and brief Jessica,' said Bec. 'We'll need a warrant for Moses' property at the airstrip. JJ needs to be found and I want to know why his vehicle was at Valhalla Railway Station on the morning of the bombing.'

61

JJ was mixing dichloroacetylene in the coolroom built into the rear corner of the aircraft hangar when he heard a car approaching. He strode from the coolroom, closing the door behind him, and went over to the access door of the hangar. He looked out and saw Bobby Brown's old Chevy speeding towards him. The car skidded to a stop and Bobby jumped out.

'We've got to get out of here. They're onto you.'

'Did you tell them I'd be here,' said JJ. 'You're dead if you did.'

'No way, man. I said you're living at your father's place. We gotta get outta here.'

'Don't worry. The plane's fuelled up and ready to go. We're going to Florida first, and then we'll catch a commercial flight to South America. But first, one more job.'

'No JJ, let's get outta here.'

'We will. But not yet. Come with me.' Bobby followed JJ as he moved to the rear of the hangar. 'Help me take off this tarpaulin.'

Bobby saw the shape of a White-GMC front loading garbage truck. 'Not another garbage truck.' He stared at JJ. 'You gotta be joking.'

'Come on,' JJ said aggressively. He grabbed Bobby's arm and pulled him over to the truck. Together they removed the tarpaulin.

'Alright, now I want the remaining bags of ANFO in the back of the truck.'

Bobby looked at the fifty bags of ANFO packed against the wall of the hanger. 'JJ, no.'

JJ grabbed his old infantry buddy's jacket and pulled him close. 'Listen, you gutless piece of shit. I said one more job.' He jerked Bobby's jacket, pulling him even closer. 'And that's what's going to happen. Move the ANFO to the rear of the truck.'

Bobby started sulking but began lifting bags onto a trolley. It took five trips to move them to the rear of the vehicle. Together, they lifted individual bags into the rear bin of the garbage truck, and then JJ carefully stacked them. An hour later, covered in sweat, they finished loading the explosives.

'Alright, start the truck,' JJ told Bobby.

Brown climbed into the driver's seat while JJ clambered up behind the cabin and looked down into the hopper, checking that the packing plate was in position to push rubbish into the bin.

'Bobby, slowly move the packing plate to the rear of the truck. I want to make sure it's in the right position to seal the bin. But do it slowly. I don't want the plate pushing against the ANFO and setting off an explosion.'

JJ watched Bobby push a switch on the centre consul fitted between the dash and the seats to activate the packing plate. The truck's hydraulic motor came to life and the packing plate moved slowly to the rear of the truck. 'Stop there,' he yelled. The plate sealed the end of the rubbish container.

'Alright, leave the rear gate up, but turn off the truck.'

Bobby Brown climbed out of the cabin and lit a joint. JJ left him moping near the truck and went over to the bench. He still had the detonator to sort out.

62

Bec climbed into bed in the four-star motel one mile from the FBI offices at Woodland Park in New Jersey. Fatigue had spread through her body and mind. The team had spent most of the day activating the largest operations room at Woodland Park. She needed sleep before the planned raid. A large house, aeroplane hangar, shed and fifty acres of land had to be checked and searched for JJ, Shehadeh, Lucy Donaldson and the missing dump truck. Briefing agents about JJ, Shehadeh and Lucy Donaldson had also taken time. She'd stressed they were probably armed, as the same gun had killed Officer Lehman and old Joe, the owner of the missing truck.

The command vehicle would be positioned at the front gate of the property to co-ordinate the operation and feed information back to Woodland Park. Jessica White would be forward commander. Bec, Musa and Gerry Gomez would also be positioned at the front gate and would act as a small reserve group. Two ambulances would be stationed five minutes away.

SWAT and Hostage Rescue Teams had flown to Newark International Airport from the FBI's centre at Quantico. They commandeered a hangar to plan the raid. The teams would fly to the property using night vision and land at each end of the airstrip before dawn. SWAT certified agents from Bec's office in Manhattan had driven to the airport in a BearCat armoured vehicle to meet the two helicopters when they flew into Newark.

Satellite images showed there were no other roads entering or leaving the property. The BearCat would enter the acreage through the main gate as the helicopters dropped trained agents on the airstrip. The SWAT team would break into the house and the Hostage Rescue Team would support them if a siege situation developed.

Special Agent Blum had based himself at Woodland Park to supply regular briefings to the FBI Director. The possibility that a Senator's daughter was involved with Shehadeh was politically very sensitive. Bec knew the director would provide information to the Attorney General as the operation progressed.

The raid was scheduled for five in the morning. Bec saw the digital clock move past midnight and turned over and tried to sleep. Musa crashed in the next room. He'd been just as busy and grumpier than usual. He was unhappy with Jessica's decision to keep them together at the forward command vehicle. He was trained for SWAT duties, and he'd made it clear he wanted to use that training.

Bec bounded out of bed at ten to three. Sometime after midnight, she'd managed to fall asleep. Now she was wide awake and keen to get the raid started. She quickly dressed and went to the bathroom. At three o'clock, the alarm she'd set on her phone sounded. She still had a bit of time, but adrenalin was moving through her body, and she didn't want to stay in the room any longer.

Musa was waiting in the passage.

'How are you doing?' he asked.

'Couldn't sleep.'

'Yeah, I kept waking up. Coffee?'

'Okay, let's grab one and get this show on the road.'

They moved quietly to the lobby. Both grabbed large black coffees from the machine, and they carried them to the parking lot with their gear. Bec climbed in the passenger seat, and Musa drove them to the office at Woodland Park. Neither spoke.

When they entered the operations room, Jessica White was already there fiddling with some paperwork.

'Did you get any sleep?' asked Bec.

'I stayed here drinking coffee. Surveillance reported a vehicle going onto the property at 0323 hours.'

'Whose vehicle was it?' asked Bec.

'Not sure. We think it was Tomlin's BMW. Surveillance was too far away.'

'Tomlin Junior would be driving it,' said Musa. 'The old man's dead.'

'You guys ready?' asked Jessica.

'Yep,' Bec replied. Her voice was strong, confident.

They jumped in their vehicles and drove towards Moses' private airstrip in the woods near Stokes State Forest. The helicopter with the SWAT team would land at the northern end of the airstrip, the end closest to the house. The Hostage Rescue Team would land at the southern end. The

BearCat armoured vehicle would go through the main gate. Local police would stop vehicles entering the road leading to the property.

63

Bec drove their unmarked vehicle and led the convoy to Richard Moses' property. She was followed by the forward command vehicle and the BearCat. They stopped on the road that passed the property and airstrip. It was a sheltered spot under some trees. Bec made sure that their position could not be seen from the house. She looked at her watch. It was 0450 and still dark, but the sky to the east was starting to lighten.

'Gomez has the bolt cutters,' Bec said quietly to Musa. 'I'm going with him to see if the front gate is locked. You help set up the forward command vehicle.'

He whispered back to her. 'Will do. Be careful.'

The gate was secured with a padlock and chain, but the arm length bolt cutters Gomez had brought with him made short work of snapping through the chain. Bec eased the gate open, ready for the BearCat to drive through.

She heard the two helicopters approaching and knew they would touch down at exactly 0500 hours. The pilots would keep the helicopter rotors turning. It would take less than thirty seconds for the SWAT and Hostage Rescue Teams to jump from them and take defensive positions in the tree line.

The morning light was increasing, so Bec moved into the tree line and found a position where she could see the closest helicopter. She heard the change of sound in the helicopter's twin engines as it prepared to fly back to the designated field two minutes away. They were on schedule.

'Trip wire!' a voice yelled through her two-way radio. Bec saw it but it was too late.

The huge Sikorsky UH-60 Black Hawk helicopter lifted and moved forward as the pilot increased the speed of the rotors. The front left landing wheel caught and pulled on a wire that Bec could see crossing the airstrip at knee height. Noise and light filled the dawn air as the blast hit the helicopter. Bec froze as it pitched into the air, held its position for a moment then crashed onto its side. The spinning rotor blades hit the ground and sheared off. She saw one blade skimming across the ground just missing a SWAT team member and burying itself into a tree trunk.

Bec heard the pilot screaming and turned to see fire devouring the aircraft. She started running towards the burning monster, but the flames forced her back. She turned and ran towards the command vehicle. She could see the big BearCat was on its way to the airstrip.

'Trip wires,' she yelled into her handset. 'Take cover. All agents take cover and don't move.'

Musa was standing at the gate. As she reached him, she heard a popping sound from somewhere near the armoured vehicle. Musa was suddenly wrapping his arms around her and pushing his body against hers. She fell backwards with Musa on top of her as the BearCat lifted into the air and fell on its side.

Bec was on the ground with Musa on top of her. She was stunned and her ears were ringing. She eased herself from under Musa's unconscious body and fought back tears as she took his wrist and felt for a pulse.

'Is he okay?' Jessica yelled, running towards them.

'He's got a pulse. He's breathing. I'm checking for injuries.

'Okay, look after him. I'm checking the BearCat.'

She kept talking as she looked and felt for any obvious injuries.

'Musa, it's going to be alright. You're going to be fine. Hang in there.'

She could find no signs of bleeding, but she knew damage from the blast could be internal.

In her radio, she could hear Jessica talking to Woodland Park.

'We've got two teams taking cover after explosions. Both have casualties. The BearCat and its crew are out of action. We need reinforcements and more ambulances.'

Bec cradled Musa's head in her lap.

'Are you alright?' Jessica asked, when she got back from the BearCat.

'I'm good. Are the ambulances coming?'

'They won't be long.'

But Bec was far from alright. She had a massive headache, her ears were ringing, and she was making sure her partner, who had saved her life, was still breathing.

64

JJ's eyes were closed but he was awake and fully clothed when he heard a helicopter motor in the distance. He wasn't overly concerned, as helicopters were often in the sky, but he knew what it meant when he heard the motor of a second helicopter: they were coming to his airstrip.

He was running from his bedroom when Bobby Brown rushed from the bedroom next door.

'Let's get out of here,' said Bobby.

JJ grabbed his shirt. 'Come with me.'

They left the house through the sliding doors of the entertainment room and moved quietly to the access door of the hangar.

The hangar had the usual large sliding doors at the front, but a large roller door was fitted at the back. When the hangar was built, the rear roller door accessed a dirt track, which was the original route to the house. The new road on the other side of the property now allowed better access to the airstrip.

JJ heard the two helicopters hovering, and then an explosion ripped through the air.

'What was that?' asked Bobby.

'What do think? Start the truck.'

JJ went to the storeroom and unlocked the door. Paul Shehadeh and Lucy Donaldson were bound and gagged on the floor. He cut Lucy's leg ties.

'Get up,' he said, dragging her to her feet.

He pulled her to the rear of the garbage truck, where the tailgate had been left open after they loaded the explosives, and then pushed her. 'Get in.'

Lucy climbed on top of the white bags. JJ turned and saw Bobby staring.

'What's she doing here?' Bobby stammered.

JJ pulled his Glock pistol from his belt holster and pointed it at Bobby. 'Watch her or the end of this barrel is the last thing you will see.'

He returned to the storeroom and cut Shehadeh's leg ties.

'Get up,' he said, pointing the Glock at Shehadeh.

Shehadeh stood up. JJ grabbed the back of his collar and pointed the Glock at his head. 'Move.'

JJ steered him towards the rear of the garbage truck and then made him climb onto the white bags next to Lucy. He handed some plastic ties to Bobby.

'Put these around their ankles.'

Bobby sulked off with the plastic ties and climbed into the rear of the garbage truck. JJ waved his pistol at him. 'Hurry up,' he said.

Bobby finished fitting the ties and jumped from the truck.

'Watch them while I close the tailgate,' said JJ. He moved to the truck's cabin, jumped in and pushed the switch fitted to the centre console between the seats. Hydraulics hissed into life and lowered the heavy metal tailgate, closing Paul and Lucy in the darkening rear bin.

As it closed, another explosion was heard in the distance.

'Get the roller door, Bobby, and drop the fence.'

Bobby went to the rear exit of the hangar and pulled the chain. The door rattled up, and JJ moved the gear lever to first and edged the truck forward. Bobby cut the wire holding the fence behind the hangar. When it dropped, Bobby rushed to the slow-moving truck and jumped into the cabin. JJ edged the truck forward and drove over the fence that was lying on the ground.

Over the years, shrubs had grown from the dirt of the original track. And the branches of red oaks, tulip trees and black spruce made a canopy over what remained of the rough, dirt road. Even in winter, the bare tree limbs made it difficult to spot the track from the air and from Google Earth satellites. JJ had cut down a few shrubs and low hanging branches over the last three months and strategically placed white paint on trees to mark the route for driving at night without lights.

In under three minutes, after checking the route with the torch on his smartphone when needed, JJ turned onto the local road and switched on his headlights. Anyone who spotted the vehicle would not be concerned at seeing a garbage truck early in the morning.

JJ stayed on back roads and headed north, driving for an hour to Sterling Forest. As the sun was starting to warm the tops of the trees, he drove into a sheltered clearing not far from the quarry where he had found the cache of explosives.

'What are you doing?' whined Bobby. 'We've got to get out of here.'

'We will, but not until dark. They'll have helicopters buzzing around everywhere.'

65

Bec was still at the airstrip, which was crawling with FBI agents and Marines from the Corps Base at Quantico, when Jessica White returned to her. Musa and the other casualties had been airlifted to the Hackensack University medical hospital at Bergen, New Jersey. Bec had recovered from the initial shock, but her body was bruised and sore.

They moved to the hangar and saw the open roller door at the rear and truck tyre marks in the dirt.

'I bet that's old Joe's second garbage truck,' said Bec. 'And Shehadeh and JJ will be in it.'

'Well, if Shehadeh and Tomlin Junior are in the truck, what about Lucy? Where would she be?'

'Lucy will be with Shehadeh,' she said, 'and the person who might know where they're going is Rosa Flores. Let's get out of here and talk to her.'

66

B ec and Jessica walked from the FBI offices in Federal
Plaza to the CIA offices in Lower Manhattan. Bec
had contacted Tony Flores and requested to speak to his
daughter, Rosa. Surveillance of Lucy showed that Rosa
had less contact with her after the pair attended a meeting at Americans for Palestine. Bec wanted to know about
Lucy and Rosa's relationship and Rosa's knowledge of
Shehadeh.

Tony Flores greeted them and took them to an interview room where Rosa was waiting for them. He remained
in the room while Bec spoke to his daughter.

'Rosa, I understand you are a student at Columbia
University?'

'Yes.'

'What are you studying?'

'Computer engineering.'

'You attended Middle Eastern Studies as an elective, is
that correct?'

'Yes.'

'Why did you choose that elective?'

Rosa looked at her father, and he nodded.

'I'm a CIA intern. I saw Paul Shehadeh's name on an

unclassified file and I thought it would be interesting to attend his class.'

'How did you meet Lucy Donaldson?'

'On the first day of Middle Eastern Studies. We sat together.'

'You became friends?'

'Yes.'

'What about Paul Shehadeh. Did you become friendly with him?'

'Not really. Lucy was keen to make friends with him, and I was with Lucy a lot of the time early on.'

'Do you think Lucy has become involved with Shehadeh?'

'Yes.'

'Did they become lovers?'

'Lucy talked about wanting to get into bed with him, but I don't know. She never told me if they did. We started to drift apart.'

'Do you know anything about the bombing at Kensico Reservoir?'

'No, I was shocked when it happened. Dad and I talked about it, but I don't know anything that wasn't in the news.'

'Paul Shehadeh, could he be involved in the bombing?'

'Paul involved...?' Rosa looked at Bec and then her father.

'You look surprised. Do you think he could be involved?'

'I don't know. He was always talking about a lack of water in Palestine and how much water we have in America, but I wouldn't think so. He didn't know many people in America, and he would have needed help.'

'If there was another attack on New York's water supply,

what would be the likely target? What would Shehadeh choose to hit?'

Rosa's eyes opened wide and Bec watched her thinking. After a little while, she said, 'He always talked about water infrastructure around New York, and Lucy mentioned going to Kensico Reservoir with him. They played golf at Van Cortlandt Park where there's the new valve chamber and filtration plant. He mentioned that a few times. He wanted to visit but couldn't get approval.' She thought for a while. 'And he wanted to visit the tunnelling for Pipeline 3.'

'The new pipeline that's going to supply water to Manhattan?'

'Yes.'

Bec changed tack.

'Do you know where Lucy could be?'

Rosa shook her head. 'No.'

'Did you know Shehadeh has gone missing?'

'I thought something must have happened. Middle Eastern Studies is getting a new lecturer, but Dad told me to keep my head down and not ask questions until Paul and Lucy are found.'

'Do you think Lucy is with Shehadeh?'

'Probably.'

'What about Lucy, was she involved in the Kensico bombing?'

'I wouldn't think so, but I really don't know.'

67

Storm clouds gathered over Sterling Forest as the evening approached. When night finally arrived, an intense black canopy was above them. Bobby Brown had whined in JJ's ear several times during the day about using the dark to make a run for it. He was all for leaving the truck and getting out of there.

JJ had other plans.

Just after midnight, JJ finished his joint and stubbed the remains.

'Alright, it's time. Start the truck.'

Bobby jumped into the cabin and turned the key. The diesel clattered into life.

'Open the tailgate,' said JJ.

Bobby pushed the switch on the centre console. The hydraulics activated two pistons. The heavy metal tailgate, which was hinged at the top of the bin, opened slowly, exposing Paul and Lucy. Both were still bound and lying on the bags of ANFO. JJ pulled Paul from the rear of the truck, and he fell to the ground. JJ pulled out his pistol and pointed it at him while cutting his leg ties with his free hand.

'Get up,' he ordered.

As Paul stood up, JJ put the pistol to his head and yanked him to the side of the truck.

'Watch her,' he yelled to Bobby, who was climbing out of the cabin.

JJ pushed Shehadeh to the passenger door of the vehicle. 'Get in. I want you with me in the cabin. This time, you're not just going to be a bomber, you're going to be a suicide bomber. That might help the cops solve the case.'

Shehadeh climbed into the cabin using his tied hands to pull himself into the compartment.

'Okay, on the floor with your head on the seat.' Shehadeh knelt on the floor facing the rear of the cabin and put his head down.

'Bobby, jump in and close the tailgate.'

Bobby jumped into the cabin and activated the hydraulics while JJ watched both Shehadeh and the tailgate, making sure Lucy did not escape.

'Okay, come around here and put a tie around his ankles. I don't want him running off on me.'

Bobby moved from the driver's seat to the passenger door and slipped a plastic tie around Shehadeh's ankles. Then, he stared at JJ. 'Where am I going to sit?'

JJ smiled. 'You want out of here. Well, you're getting out of here.' He reached behind his back and produced the Arabian dagger. JJ enjoyed seeing the look of fear on Bobby's face. He thrust the curved blade forward and Bobby grunted as the steel moved into his abdomen. JJ pulled upwards with the knife, opening a long wound in Bobby's body. Intestines fell from the open laceration, almost reaching the ground. Bobby grabbed two handfuls of his entrails and tried to return them to their warm home, but the large muscular tube kept slipping through his bloodied hands. His strength waned and Bobby slipped onto the forest floor.

JJ saw Shehadeh staring at him through the open door of the cabin.

'You're next,' he said, and slammed shut the passenger door.

After climbing back into the cabin, JJ drove from Sterling Forest and headed east. He could see Shehadeh's head in the light of the instrument panel. He was still on his knees on the floor of the cabin with his face resting on the passenger seat.

'You know, if those deadhead cops had any brains, you'd be in jail by now. I couldn't have done anymore to show them you did the bombing at Kensico Dam. But that doesn't matter now.'

At two in the morning, he slowed as he approached Van Cortlandt Park. All looked quiet. The filtration plant was in the south-eastern corner. He turned off Jerome Avenue and drove towards it. JJ looked at Shehadeh, who was still on his knees.

'If you move, you're dead.'

JJ steered towards the pop-up bollards in front of the entrance gate. They were new, and he wondered if he should reverse out. He decided to continue. He pulled up just short of the bollards and tooted the horn. The security guard stepped from his small office and approached the truck. JJ lowered the driver's window and looked down at the guard.

'Rubbish collection,' he said.

The guard frowned. 'Let me check.'

'I'm running late. Can you hurry up?'

'You'll get in when I'm good and ready,' the guard replied. 'Have you got any paperwork?'

'Sure, it's here somewhere.'

He leaned forward as if looking for some paperwork. As he did, he pulled his Glock from its holster on his belt. He reached across his body with his right hand.

'Here's the paperwork,' he said, and poked the Glock through the open driver's window and pulled the trigger.

The noise of the shot echoed across the park. The guard stumbled back, still looking at JJ, and fell to the ground.

'Sleep tight,' said JJ, as he placed the pistol on his lap. He pushed the gear lever into reverse and drove back a short distance before swinging on the steering wheel to turn around. He engaged first gear and drove from the entrance road, turned right onto Jerome Avenue and headed south, watching for flashing lights. After five minutes, he looked over to Shehadeh.

'Well lover boy, we couldn't get into the filtration plant. Let's move to Plan B, shall we?'

JJ saw Shehadeh looking back at him, so he reached over and hit his head with the bottom of his fist.

'What do you think you're looking at?' Shehadeh closed his eyes and turned his head towards the passenger door.

'That's better.'

68

Bec Bekele woke to the sound of The Troggs singing Wild Thing on her cell phone. She gently moved Jessica White's arm, which was draped over her body holding her tight. She reached over to the table at the side of the bed.

'Hello?'

'Bec, it's the ops centre. A security guard has been shot at the entrance to Van Cortlandt Park valve chamber and filtration plant. There's CCTV vision of a garbage truck at the entrance gate when he was shot.'

'Jesus!'

Bec quickly moved to work mode.

'Get onto Assistant Commissioner Anderson from the Department of Environmental Conservation. Tell him what happened and ask if he can get their helicopter up in the air. Their people would have a better idea of the important water infrastructure around New York.'

'They already know what's going on. It was their security guard.'

'Of course. Okay, ask if their helicopter can pick us up at Downtown Manhattan heliport in forty-five minutes.'

Bec ended the call.

'What happened?' asked Jessica, still half asleep.

'There's been a shooting at Van Cortlandt Park valve chamber. A security guard has been killed … and a garbage truck was at the gate.'

69

The DEP helicopter was waiting with its engine running and blades turning ready for take-off. As they jumped in, Bec saw a stressed looking Assistant Commissioner Anderson.

'I thought I better join you,' he said.

There were no light-hearted comments to Bec this time, and she noted he had aged and lost weight. She saw that the comfortable roundness in his body was no longer there.

After five minutes, they were flying over Van Cortlandt Park. There were flashing lights everywhere.

'The scene has been sealed off. Everything is contained. The valve chamber and the filtration plant are secure,' said Anderson through the headsets. NYPD is also keeping a lookout for the truck, but it hasn't been sighted.'

'They've had a go at Kensico and now Van Cortlandt Park,' said Bec. 'What about Pipeline 3? Can a truckload of explosives get to the pipeline with the upgraded security?'

'We've got Kensico covered. No-one is allowed to enter Kensico Plaza, and more blocks of concrete have been placed to stop access to the dam wall. Van Cortlandt Park is even more secure. The new bollards did their job at the main gate. Pipeline 3 is a bit harder. Security at the entrances to the tunnel for the pipeline has been beefed up since the Kensico bombing, but construction work is continuing. Work trucks are entering the tunnel all the time.'

'Let's check out each of the entrances,' responded Bec.

The pilot flew and hovered above each entrance into the tunnel. The strobe lights of two NYPD cars flashed at each one.

'We've called for assistance from the military, as well,' said the assistant commissioner, as the helicopter flew over Central Park after inspecting the last entrance. 'Explosive experts are on the way.'

Bec thought about the attempted attack at Van Cortlandt Park.

'What happens if power to the valve chamber and filtration plant at Van Cortlandt Park goes down?'

'Backup generators kick in to keep essential computers and control panels working, but the water supply will drop to a trickle after four hours. Things get tricky after that if we don't restore power.'

'Where does the plant get their mains power?'

'Mott Haven sub-station in the Bronx.'

'Let's have a look there.'

'Okay,' said the assistant commissioner. 'It's worth a look.' He directed the pilot to Bruckner Boulevard in Mott Haven.

'Have you got FLIR on the helicopter?' asked Bec.

'Yes, why?'

'Ask the pilot to activate the infrared camera and to fly high with lights off.'

'Sir,' said the pilot to his assistant commissioner. 'I'm not sure I can do that. Air traffic regulations ban that sort of thing.'

'Look,' Bec forcefully replied, 'there is a truck bomb down there that's trying to take out New York's water supply. If the bombers see us, they might detonate the bomb in a crowded place. Turn off the lights.'

The pilot hesitated. Assistant Commissioner Anderson's voice came across in the headsets. 'Turn off the lights. It's on me if there's a complaint.'

'Yes sir.'

70

JJ drove the garbage truck into St Mary's Park in the Bronx, less than five minutes away from Mott Haven electricity sub-station, stopping the truck near two dumpster bins at the rear of the building housing the recreation centre. He lowered the driver's window to halfway and turned off the motor and lights. The park was quiet. The morning birds had not yet started their calls. Faint traffic noises could be heard on Bruckner Boulevard in the distance.

'Just calling in to pick up the rubbish,' he said, looking down at Shehadeh. 'Nothing unusual about that, is there?'

He reached behind his seat and pulled a bag onto his lap. Opening the zipper, he took out a small, cheap WESE BM10 cell phone. He set its vibrating alarm to activate in forty-five minutes, then he carefully removed a detonator from a hard case normally used for glasses and cautiously taped it to the phone.

Shehadeh was watching every move.

'Not long now, lover boy,' said JJ.

JJ restarted the truck's motor and once again pushed a switch on the centre console. The packing plate in the hopper moved towards the vehicle's cabin. He jumped from the cabin and climbed to the top of the hopper. He shone the torchlight of his smart phone into the hopper and could see Lucy still bound on top of ANFO bags in the rear bin. He then carefully placed the WESE phone with the detonator taped to it between two bags of ANFO.

He said to Lucy. 'Don't worry. You and your boyfriend won't feel a thing.'

JJ dropped from the side of the hopper onto the asphalt before mounting the two steps on the side of the truck to jump back into the cabin. He sat in the driver's seat and reached for the control switch. Again, the pneumatic pump whirled, and the packing plate screeched and scraped back so that it would be impossible for Lucy to escape.

He switched on the truck's lights, engaged first gear and drove from the rear of St Mary's Recreation Center. JJ turned left on St Ann's Avenue and headed to Mott Haven substation. He approached the gate of the complex and stopped. The gate slid sideways, and JJ drove slowly forward to the entrance gate to the substation. By now, it was five o'clock in the morning, but there was no other traffic.

JJ worked the controls. The large arm assembly that lifted dumpster bins up and over the cabin came alive. He eased the tongues of the fork between the bars of the gate and started lifting it upwards. A screeching noise pierced the early morning quiet as the tongues moved against the metal gate. There weren't any residents nearby, but JJ worried how far the noise would carry.

The hydraulic arms easily handled the weight of the gate. It rose slowly into the air, steadied by the large metal posts that kept it upright. But as soon as it was free from its guideposts, the gate shifted. JJ quickly adjusted the controls, and the gate balanced for an instant before it toppled and crashed to the ground. He watched the corner of the gate hit the ground and fall sideways against the door on his side of the truck.

JJ stared at the gate. 'Shit.'

Then, in the corner of his eye, he saw movement. He turned to see Shehadeh fiddling with the controls that operated the packing plate. JJ swung his fist to hit him, but Shehadeh pulled away and jumped from the truck's cabin.

'You bastard,' he yelled, ignoring the scraping of the metal packing plate as he scrambled over the truck's high centre console.

Shehadeh had fallen to the ground and was struggling to pull off his leg ties.

'You won't be breaking those,' said JJ, jumping from the cabin. As he did, the pistol in his belt caught on the seatbelt and fell to the ground. Shehadeh pushed himself to his feet, completed a two-legged hop and reached for it. JJ swung his right leg and kicked him in the ribs. Shehadeh grunted and fell away from the weapon.

JJ kicked the gun away and sucked in the cool morning air.

'I've had enough of you,' he said and reached behind his back and pulled his father's khanjar from the sheath tucked into his belt.

'You people like cutting off heads. Let's see how you like it.'

Crouching slightly, JJ moved behind Paul and grabbed a handful of his black hair. He pulled Paul's head back, exposing the brown skin of his throat and then lifted the dagger. The bright lights of the compound reflected off its curved blade.

71

Lucy was stiff and sore. She wasn't sure how long she'd been in the back of the garbage truck, but it had to be hours. She'd managed to bring her hands to the front of her body by stretching her arms down her back and below her butt, raising her knees to her chin and then easing her hands over her feet. But her hands and feet were still tied. She rolled over onto her other side to ease a pain in her shoulder. As she moved into a comfortable position, the pneumatic motor hissed. The metal packing plate scraped back allowing fresh air and the light of a streetlamp into her solid metal cell. The light reflected off something and caught her eye. She wondered what it could be and if it might be useful. Refreshed by the air and light, she thought of escaping for the first time since she'd been trapped in the truck.

Lucy was about to drag herself to the reflecting object when she heard a noise from the side of the hopper. She quickly dropped back down and kept still. She watched as her captor eased himself into the back of the truck and reach down between two of the bags. When he turned his smart phone light towards her, she closed her eyes and prayed he'd leave her alone. It was only when she heard him pulling himself out that she dared open her eyes again.

When she was first placed in the truck's bin, Lucy had seen the warning signs on the bags. At first she'd panicked at every jolt of the truck. Now, she was wondering what the guy had been doing with the bags. Then, the realisation hit her, and her mind screamed. He'd put a detonator between the bags.

Lucy desperately pulled herself toward the location where her captor bent down. She was nearly there when the hydraulic noise started again, and the packing plate slowly started to close her into her prison.

She scrambled to the bags where she thought the detonator was placed. Her fingers felt for it, but it wasn't there. Desperate, Lucy felt her way forward to another pair of bags. She felt between them, and her fingers touched a cell phone with the detonator taped to it. The black, dirty plate continued towards her, scratching metal against metal. With her two bound hands, Lucy tossed the phone up towards the narrowing opening. The phone flew towards the space, hitting the rim at the top of the bin just as the packing plate shut out the light. She felt for the phone and detonator but couldn't find it.

Lucy collapsed onto the bags of explosive and tears came to her eyes. She lay there exhausted. Then, she remembered the reflection when the light entered her cell. She was in a garbage truck. There had to be something that could cut the plastic ties. She started feeling around the edges where things might get trapped. She knew she'd found what she wanted when she cut her finger on something trapped between the wall of the truck and the big moving metal plate. It felt like a flattened metal can. She ignored her bleeding finger and started sawing the plastic ties around her wrists. It seemed to take an eternity, but eventually it cut through. Lucy pulled the can from where it was jammed and was cutting at her ankle ties when she heard the now familiar hydraulic sound and the scraping of metal as the packing plate started moving again. Light appeared. She quickened her pace and cut through the last plastic tie. With her hands and legs free, she scurried over to the opening and pulled herself from the back of the truck.

When she jumped to the ground, Lucy could hear some shouting on the other side of the vehicle. She crept to the front of the truck and poked her head around. Paul was lying on the ground. She was about to go to him when the guy from the classroom walked into view. He kicked a gun across the ground and walked towards Paul, looking like a predator stalking its prey. He grabbed Paul by the hair, pulled his head back and put the blade of a dagger to his throat.

'No!' she yelled.

Lucy saw the surprised look on the predator's face as she ran towards them. She hit him at full speed and heard the clang of the dagger hitting the ground. But she lost her grip on him when they hit the asphalt surface and rolled apart.

Lucy tried to stand but was too stunned, and his swinging arm hit her in the temple.

'I'll fix you later,' he said, and turned back to Paul.

Lucy lay on the ground trying to recover. She could see the gun her captor had kicked aside. She forced herself to her feet and struggled to the weapon. She lifted it from the ground and pointed it at Paul's attacker, who was grabbing his hair with the dagger in his hand.

The gun waved around at the end of her arm. She felt a wave of fear and her legs shook. But she forced herself to shout out.

'Stop!'

He hesitated and looked at her. His eyes narrowed when he saw the gun in her hand.

'Well, look at you. Lover girl has a gun. You're going to save your boyfriend now?'

He pushed Paul to the ground and started striding towards her. Lucy heard the explosion and felt the kickback of the gun in her hand. The guy stopped and looked down at his body. But Lucy couldn't see any blood. She'd missed.

Paul yelled to her. 'Two hands, Lucy. Two hands.'

Lucy moved her left hand to support the weapon underneath the trigger guard. She squeezed the trigger and saw the guy touch his right shoulder. He looked at the blood on his fingers and then smiled at her.

Anger overwhelmed her. 'You bastard!' she cried.

Lucy squeezed the trigger three more times. The bullets hit higher and higher up the guy's body as the gun in her hands lifted from the recoil. The last bullet hit him in his right eye, and bits of brain and bone flew from the back of his head. There was a rumble of thunder as he collapsed to the ground and the dagger fell from his grip and landed at his side.

Lucy's anger left her, and tears welled in her eyes. She began to tremble, then her body started shaking uncontrollably. Her legs buckled, and she slipped to her knees as if in prayer, holding the gun in the two-handed grip Paul had shown her at the shooting range.

She was still kneeling as first rays of sunshine broke through the clouds, ending her nightmare. Through her tears, she watched Paul cut his ties with the dagger and walk over to her. He took the gun from her hands and held her tight.

72

Paul Shehadeh found it painful to hold Lucy. His ribs were broken, and he could taste blood in his mouth. But he wasn't going to let go of the woman who saved his life.

He could hear the distinctive whoop, whoop, whoop of helicopter blades getting louder. The helicopter descended and hovered over the parking lot. Two people jumped from it. They ran towards him with guns drawn. He saw the FBI vests and heard them yelling.

'Drop the weapon. Drop the weapon.'

Paul Shehadeh threw the Glock towards the garbage truck. At the same moment there was an explosion and a flash of light.

Paul covered Lucy with his body. The two people running towards him hit the ground and the helicopter rose into the sky. A few seconds later, he looked around. They were still alive, the truck was in one piece, but the remains of a phone were scattered on the ground. He realised Lucy must have found the phone and detonator when he activated the packing plate, and she'd thrown it out of the bin and away from the bags of explosives.

The two agents lifted themselves from the ground and ran towards them.

'Hands in the air. Hands in the air.'

Paul let go of Lucy and raised his hands. 'She's in shock,' he said.

He was pushed to the ground and handcuffed. More blood surged from his mouth and bubbled on the ground. He watched them do the same to Lucy, but at least they were more gentle placing her face on the asphalt.

Special Agent Robert Blum arrived at Mott Haven electric substation as Bec was about to step into the ambulance taking Paul Shehadeh to the Mt Sinai Hospital. Jessica White had already left with Lucy in another ambulance. Media helicopters were circling overhead, and a media pack was being corralled on Bruckner Drive by FBI media liaison, waiting to interview Blum.

'I need to speak with media in ten minutes,' said Blum. 'Give me a quick rundown of what happened here.'

They moved away from the open rear doors of the ambulance, and Bec quickly told him what happened.

'So that clears Shehadeh then?'

'Musa always thought he was being set up,' said Bec. 'But what if Shehadeh was involved in the Kensico Bombing and JJ double crossed him with this second bombing attempt?'

'Hmm, we can't take any chances, or stories of his involvement will start spreading on social media, and our agency will come under scrutiny. The Attorney-General will be asking how the FBI knows Shehadeh is telling the truth. So, we've got to prove what he is saying is fact ... Bec, treat Shehadeh as a suspect until we can clearly prove his innocence.'

'Yes sir.'

73

B ec was still wearing her FBI vest when the uniformed police officer from NYPD gave her the nod to enter Shehadeh's room at Mt Sinai Hospital on Madison Avenue.

'How are you?' she said.

He glanced at the handcuffs shackling him to the bed. His slight movement caused him to grimace and move his free hand to his side.

'I'll be better once these come off.'

'I'm Agent Bekele from New York's FBI office. Do you want to talk?'

'You work with Musa Halmat?'

'Yes, he's my partner.'

'He didn't believe me when I rang and told him I was being set up.'

'I'm not so sure about that. Anyway, he was just doing his job. He asked you to come in.'

'Where is he?'

'He's in hospital just like you. There were explosions at the airstrip.'

Shehadeh nodded. 'I heard the explosions. Is he alright?'

Bec looked at him. She wondered if he really cared about Musa's condition. Then she replied, 'He'll be okay.'

'I suppose I am going to be blamed for that, as well?'

Bec stared at him for a moment before replying. 'Not if we believe Lucy. She told us her version of what happened. But we need to double check your stories.'

Paul looked out the hospital window. 'She saved my life.'

'She certainly did. She's one tough girl.'

'Lucy is good. A fine young woman.'

'The doctors told me you have two fractured ribs and a punctured left lung. They expect you'll be in hospital for five days. In the meantime, we need to take various swabs and samples from you. You don't mind, do you?'

Paul half smiled. 'Agent Bekele, do I have any choice?'

Bec kept a straight face. 'Not if you want to get out of here.'

Bec grabbed a coffee and watched the crime scene investigators take samples from Shehadeh: hair for DNA and for future comparisons of hair found at any of the crime scenes, blood for DNA as well as for the testing for the presence of alcohol and drugs, dirt and any other matter was scraped from under his fingernails, swabs taken from his hands looking for the presence of chemicals used in explosives and additional swabs to check for gunpowder residue.

Traces of ammonium nitrate from the ANFO bags would be present but the presence of dichloroacetylene would be interesting. It wasn't present in the second truck. Presumably, the speed of their raid on the airport hadn't given them time to load it.

Shehadeh was photographed, his fingerprints taken, and his clothes seized. His clothes would be checked for traces of explosives, blood and any fibres stuck to the material. If Old Joe's blood was on his clothes, it would mean Shehadeh had some very interesting questions to answer. It would imply he was at Old Joe's when he was killed. Although, Bec now believed Musa's scepticism about Shehadeh being a suspect was justified.

Lucy had told her side of the story to Jessica and CCTV at Mott Haven had shown Paul jumping from the cabin of the truck and trying to escape before JJ kicked him. The pictures corroborated that part of Paul and Lucy's stories. It appeared JJ was setting him up for the explosion at the electrical substation and they were sure it was the same for Kensico Dam. But their boss was right; the agency had to make sure that they could demonstrate he was innocent. All checks would be pushed through the system, but it was still going to take time.

Her thoughts were interrupted by her smartphone.

'Hi, Bec, it's Tammy Crawford from West Milford Police.'

'Tammy, how's things?'

Bec remembered the good job Tammy Crawford had done at the recycling depot where Old Joe was shot and the second garbage truck taken.

'Bobby Brown has been found.'

'Where? We need to talk to him.'

'He's not talking to anyone. He's dead. He was found by a couple of hikers in Sterling Forest, stabbed in the abdomen with his insides hanging out.'

'Damn, we needed him to check out a suspect's story.'

'You're not talking about an Arab, are you?'

Bec was silent, wondering how much she could say. 'How do you know about an Arab?'

'Do you remember Officer Jacobs, who was the first to respond to Old Joe's death?'

'Yes, he was doing the log in your command vehicle when I arrived.'

'He's my best officer. He was the first to attend when we got the call about Brown's body, and he got Detective Hills to respond as well. Hills was also at Old Joe's scene. Anyway, Hills searched the body and found a note. Looks like the paper was torn from the truck's logbook.'

'Can you read it to me.'

'JJ is crazy. If anything happens to me, JJ did it. I was wrong to help him with the bombing. He wanted to set up the Arab. I don't want anything to happen to the girl. JJ is mad. It's signed Robert J Brown.'

'Tammy, you're a legend. You've made my day.'

'We're going to Bobby's place now to find some hand-writing samples and check it was his writing.'

'Great. We might have some of his writing from our raid on Tomlin's warehouse, as well. Let me know how you go. I owe you big time,' said Bec.

74

Bec was exhausted when she entered the hospital room at Hackensack University Medical Center with Jessica White. It had been a long day, and she hadn't got much sleep at the motel before the raid. This was her last job, and for her it was the most important one.

Tears filled her eyes when she saw her partner lying in the bed with a drip feeding into his arm. She gently touched the back of his hand, and he opened his eyes.

'Moose, are you okay?'

Musa blinked and said quietly, 'Don't call me Moose.'

He closed his eyes again, but Bec knew he must be okay to say that. A few moments passed before he opened his eyes again and reached out to her. 'You, okay?

'Thanks to you, I'm okay.' Bec wiped the tears from her eyes. 'Can you move?'

'I'm very stiff.'

Bec and Jessica watched him slowly move each foot and then each leg. He repeated the procedure with each arm and then moved to his fingers. 'Well, that was a blast,' said Musa with a straight face. 'Let's not do that again.'

Bec smiled her big, beautiful smile. 'I couldn't agree more.'

'All I can say is, well done, both of you,' said Jessica. 'The boss is recommending that we receive medals for Meritorious Achievement for our efforts. Musa, you will also get the FBI Star, for getting injured at the airport.'

Musa quietly scoffed. 'I wouldn't be getting that medal if Bec hadn't wanted to hug me when the bomb went off.'

Bec gave him a gentle, playful punch to the arm.

'Ouch,' he said.

'I have some good news,' said Jessica. 'The handwriting experts confirmed the note found on Bobby Brown was written by him. I think that wraps things up.'

'Not quite.' Bec looked at Musa then Jessica. 'Already, the media are saying this was a case of a disillusioned ex-soldier going off the rails, just like the Oklahoma City bombing. Well, Bobby's note said that Shehadeh was set up by JJ. I want to have a word with Richard Moses. I think he knows a lot more about all of this than he's letting on. I believe there's more to this case than a dishonourably discharged infantryman going off the rails.'

75

Paul Shehadeh was watching the television news from his bed at Mt Sinai Hospital. Al Jazeera was reporting on more demonstrations on the border between Palestine and Israel. An Israeli soldier had shot a teenager during the protests, and he'd died on the way to hospital. He turned off the sound when he heard a tap on the door.

'Hello, Paul.'

'Lucy, what a wonderful surprise. Please sit.'

He picked up the remote again and turned off the television.

'Don't try to move,' said Lucy.

'It's okay. The ribs aren't too bad now,' and he held up the plastic tubing leading from his ribcage. 'The lung's repairing itself with the help of this drain, but I have to be careful for a while longer.'

He saw the four stitches in her cheek and was about to ask how she was when Lucy's mother came into the room and stood at the foot of the bed.

'Senator Donaldson. Hello.'

'Hello Paul, my daughter insisted on seeing you.'

Lucy Donaldson leaned over and kissed his cheek before pulling a chair to the side of his bed. Paul saw she looked different, but he couldn't decide what had changed.

'How are you feeling?' he asked. 'You look well.'

'Not too bad, but I'm having nightmares about Tomlin walking towards me with a dagger. It's not the dagger but his weird smile that makes me wake up screaming. Mum has made an appointment with a specialist for me.'

'Good. That's important.'

She lifted a cardboard tray which she carried into the room. 'I brought you a coffee. Are you allowed to have one?'

'Sure.'

He drank the coffee while Lucy sat watching him. He wondered where this was going.

'Lucy, I want to thank you for saving my life.'

Lucy gave a little, uneasy laugh. 'You know, it was that two handed grip you taught me. I was shaking so much; I would have missed if I hadn't used two hands with the gun.'

Paul smiled. 'I'm pleased you remembered.'

Lucy looked at him and changed the subject.

'Paul, let me come to Palestine. I want to help.'

Paul looked at Senator Donaldson. She didn't say anything, so he returned a questioning gaze to Lucy.

'But——'

'Yes, I know you're married. It's more than that. I've spoken with Mum. I want to help in Palestine once I graduate. I want to help get better water to Palestinians. My degree finishes next year.'

Paul smiled. He could see Lucy had matured in a very short time.

'I see.' He thought for a moment about his response. 'Lucy, you are a beautiful person. You can help. But first, let me tell you a story. It's a story I've never told before.' Paul gathered his thoughts before continuing. 'I was a teenager, and a Jewish settler was commandeering a house in the West Bank. The house belonged to a friend of my grandfather. You may remember I told you that my grandfather taught me to fire a rifle.'

Paul looked at Senator Donaldson. He had a feeling that she knew this part of his story.

'Anyway, on the morning of the acquisition, I went to the roof of my grandfather's house and fired at an Israeli soldier who was protecting the new settler taking over the house. My father found out what I was doing but he was too late to stop me. He met me as I came down from the roof.'

'What did he do?'

'He was upset. Tears were in his eyes and he slapped my face.'

Paul gave a slight smile thinking of that moment. He continued. 'The slap shocked me. All my years growing up, he had never hit me. Not once. Do you know what he said?'

Lucy shook her head.

'You are not the boy I raised.'

Paul quietly repeated his words. 'You are not the boy I raised.' He nodded, thinking before continuing. 'And he slapped me again before walking away.' Paul gave another half-smile. 'I've thought of that moment many times. The first slap shocked me and I started to get angry. The second slap really made me angry.'

Paul looked at Lucy. He could see she was still listening.

'My father didn't speak to me for a week. I was very annoyed. Finally, I confronted him. I raged about the settlers taking our homes. My father remained calm and asked me how I felt when he slapped me the first time.'

Paul shook his head. 'I told him I was shocked. Then he asked how I felt when he slapped me the second time. I told him I was angry, and that I was still angry. I said that we needed to fight the Israelis. They are stealing our land. Then, he asked me how long we had been fighting the Israelis. I said to him, years, decades.'

Paul moved in his bed to ease the pain in his side.

'He asked me if it had stopped them taking our land, and then again he walked away. I stood there watching him move away, and it was only when he'd gone that I understood his message. Palestinians have been fighting Israeli expansion for decades without success. He was saying there had to be another way. That was what my father was teaching me. He waited until my anger subsided, and we talked for hours about finding a better way.'

Lucy looked at him, frowning. 'So, that's the reason you came to America?'

'Yes and no. First, we both agreed that education is important, learning is important. That is why I went to China. I also agreed to a non-violent approach. That's what my Living Water project is about. I'm trying to work with people: the Chinese, Americans, anyone who'll listen. And I did come to America to learn about desalination and directional drilling.'

Paul looked at Senator Donaldson and continued speaking.

'I sought out your stepfather. I knew he was well known for his work in desalination. But I asked him to be my supervisor because he was married to your mother. She's the reason I came to America. I wanted to use her influence, but I was wrong. That's not working with people. I used your stepfather.'

He returned his gaze to the woman sitting alongside his bed. 'And I used you, Lucy. I'm sorry. You shouldn't have gone through any of this.'

'But I want to help,' she said without hesitation. Paul saw the stubbornness in her face and demeanour. She reminded him of her mother when she questioned him about her daughter and about helping America.

'There are other ways you can help,' he said.

Lucy didn't say anything. Paul could see she was thinking. She had been through a terrible ordeal, but looking at the stitches on her face he thought the scarring from the wound would be slight.

After a while, she spoke. 'So, you want your father's way to be my way, is that it?'

'I want you to follow your own path, but not in Palestine. You are getting an education. You can help by staying in America and working with people here. You can tell everyone who will listen, and those who don't listen, what is happening in Palestine. Convince them to help my people.'

Paul Shehadeh saw that Lucy was considering what he'd said. He looked at the senator, and she gave him a mother's nod and smile.

76

Bec, Musa and Jessica sat around the table in the operation room set aside for the investigation of the bombing. The number of agents involved in the enquiry had halved and more were expected to move to other roles in the next few days.

Bec summarised what they knew. 'JJ stole the ammonium nitrate from the quarry, probably with Bobby Brown. And JJ made the dichloroacetylene at Moses' airport property to increase the size of the blasts. The caustic soda came from Industrial Chemical Supplies. A check of warehouse inventory shows that quantities of caustic soda are missing.'

Musa added to the story. 'I don't think JJ's father was involved. I believe JJ took it from the warehouse without his knowledge and his father committed suicide when he became suspicious of his son's activities.'

'Yes, that fits,' said Bec. 'It was JJ's car seen at Valhalla Railway Station on the morning of the explosion. Two people were in it. That would be JJ and Bobby. One of them stole Shehadeh's baseball cap when he was having a haircut and placed it in the cabin of the garbage truck at Kensico Reservoir to set him up.'

'JJ was a sicko. He could have done the bombing to get back at America for the dishonourable discharge. But there was no reason to set up Shehadeh. So, why did he?'

'So, what about Moses? Was JJ doing his dirty work?' Bec mused.

'I think so,' said Jessica. 'Yesterday, Tony Flores told me unofficially that Moses once worked for Mossad, Israel's intelligence and covert operations unit. There's a rumour around the intelligence community that he's still working for them, but Tony couldn't or wouldn't confirm it.'

'And who wouldn't want Shehadeh delivering water into Palestine?' asked Bec.

'The Israelis,' said Jessica and Musa in unison.

'It must be the Israelis,' said Jessica. 'Phone surveillance revealed that the Chinese thought he was becoming a problem, but all they had to do was remove him from the project. It's the Israelis who wouldn't want the project to go ahead.'

'Set up Shehadeh and the pipeline wouldn't get built,' said Musa. 'He'd be in jail in America.'

'So, Mossad may have approved an operation on Shehadeh? It's back to Moses, then?' queried Bec.

'Certainly, looks like it,' said Jessica. 'But he's shrewd. We've got phone calls and meetings he had with an ex- soldier who he employed. And he let his employee live on his country property and fly from his airstrip, that's all. We need more.'

Bec and Musa worked on their files for a week, preparing to raid Richard Moses' office at the Empire State Building. They planned to seize computer equipment and any files they thought may be relevant.

'The boss has been contacted in writing by lawyers for Moses,' said Jessica, entering the operations room. 'We are not to speak to him without his lawyer being present.'

'That's to be expected,' responded Bec.

'How's the application for a warrant to search his offices going?'

'Not good. I thought that we would find more on Moses. His lawyers are fighting our application.'

'Moses isn't going to say anything.'

'I've got an idea,' said Musa.

'I hope it's good,' said Jessica. 'We're getting nowhere with what we've got.'

'Let's rattle his cage. I can arrest him for possession of stolen artefacts and take that display dagger from his office.'

Bec looked at him. 'You're joking?' But his face said otherwise. 'You're serious, aren't you?'

'That's the way the New York police would do it,' he said.

'Interesting approach,' said Jessica, after taking a moment to think about it. 'Let me take your idea to the boss. We're not doing this without his approval.'

Bec smiled at her partner.

77

Agent Graham Jacobs drove Bec and Musa to the Empire State Building. He was retiring next week, and he asked if he could do it. It would be his last job. He remained downstairs with the vehicle and waited while Bec and Musa entered the lift that took them to Globle Logistics on the 72nd floor.

Lawyers were present when they entered the office of Richard Moses. One lawyer sat next to the display cabinet with the jewel encrusted Arabian dagger on show. The other, who appeared to be senior, stood alongside Richard Moses, who was seated behind his large desk.

'You have been advised in writing that my client does not wish to answer any questions,' said the lawyer standing beside Moses. 'My client has advised me that he employed an ex-soldier from the war in Afghanistan to help the man return to normal life in America. That is all he wishes to say.'

'I understand,' said Bec. 'However, I'm obliged to put some questions to Mr Moses. Mr Moses do you know who was responsible for the bombing at Kensico Dam on the twenty-eighth of April, this year?'

'I do not wish to answer any questions.'

'Was your employee, John Tomlin Jr, involved with the bombing?'

'My lawyer has advised me not to answer any questions. That is my right, and I will not answer any more questions.'

'Agent Bekele, unless you have a warrant, my client requests that you leave,' said the senior lawyer.

'Here is our warrant, and we will be conducting a search. But first, Agent Halmat wishes to say something.'

Musa stepped forward. 'Richard Moses, I am arresting you for possession of a stolen artefact from the National Museum of Iraq.'

Moses stared at Musa as he gave him his rights to remain silent. Musa asked him to stand up and turn around to be handcuffed. His face flushed, and his anger was palpable.

'Agent Bekele, please seize the Arabian dagger and display case,' said Musa.

The junior lawyer next to the display quickly jumped from his chair as Bec walked over.

Musa guided Richard Moses from his office.

'You can expect a formal complaint about this,' the senior lawyer said to Bec.

She followed Musa from the office. Jessica White was waiting in the reception area with five crime scene investigators who would search the premises and seize computers.

Cameras clicked and flashed as the two agents led Richard Moses from the main entrance of the Empire State Building. Reporters were jostling to be heard, asking Richard Moses questions.

'Mr Moses, is it true you are in possession of artefacts stolen from the National Museum of Iraq?'

'I have no comment to make.'

'Is it true that you once worked for Mossad, Israel's secret service?'

'I have no comment to make,' he said again, as Musa placed him in the rear seat of their vehicle.

They took him to the FBI holding cells where he was charged and then taken away to be photographed and fingerprinted.

'I wonder who tipped off the reporters?' Musa mused as they watched Moses being led from the charge room.

Bec kept a straight face. 'That's law enforcement, the FBI way.'

78

Debra Donaldson rushed into her kitchen.

'Coffee's on the bench,' said her husband, sitting at the kitchen table.

She grabbed the mug and stood in front of the kitchen window and let the morning sun warm her. The day promised bright sunshine, but with a press conference in the morning and a meeting of the Foreign Affairs Committee in the afternoon, she would not be outside enjoying it.

'Another busy day?'

'Ah ha, press conference this morning,' she said distractedly.

'Lucy will be coming with me to Columbia today,' said John Marshall. 'Her first day back.'

'She told me. I'm pleased she's starting back after everything that's happened.'

'She seems to be progressing well.'

'The doctor's happy. He said her prognosis is good.'

The senator was pleased that Lucy was recovering well from shock caused by the shooting and everything that had happened, but her innocence and youth had disappeared. When they'd visited Paul Shehadeh in the hospital, she still seemed trusting and positive about the world, but she'd grown quickly to be a mature woman: a woman similar to herself at that age.

'Paul Shehadeh left to go home, yesterday.'

'I know,' she said, her voice distant.

'What's the press conference about?'

'America's success returning stolen artefacts to the Middle East. I'm announcing the return of stolen artefacts to the National Museum of Iraq: a matching pair of khanjars.'

'The dagger Tomlin had?'

'Yes, Tomlin had one and Moses had the other. It appears that Tomlin senior brought them into the country from Iraq and sold one to Moses, who's now been arrested. That's how they met.'

'All artefacts should be returned home,' said John Marshall, as he finished his coffee.

'Yes, they should. But they're said to be cursed, as well. I'm very pleased they're leaving America.'

'What's the story behind that?'

'The smaller khanjar was a gift from a sultan to his son. But the son wanted his father's larger khanjar. So, he killed him and became sultan. Legend has it the daggers are now cursed, and whoever has them will die.'

'Didn't Tomlin commit suicide?'

'Sure did.'

'And Lucy killed JJ while he was holding the dagger.'

'I don't even want to think about it.'

'You know,' said Debra Donaldson, turning away from the window to look at her husband. 'I see the taking of the khanjars by Tomlin as symbolising everything wrong with our efforts in the Middle East in recent years. Our war in

Iraq was based on the false premise that Saddam Hussein had weapons of mass destruction. We did something that was not justified. That war in Iraq was America's khanjar moment. We are still struggling to recover our position in the Middle East because of Iraq.'

'Are you going to mention that at the press conference?'

Debra knew her husband was joking. 'No way, the Republicans would crucify me.'

'Israel won't be happy with Moses being arrested. Are they using the victim argument?'

'They are. They say the FBI is treating him unfairly. Unfortunately, the bullied have become the bullies.'

'Hmm. What's going to happen to Moses?'

'The Attorney General briefed the President about everything, including the CIA's suspicions about Moses being involved with Mossad. The President wasn't happy with the idea that Mossad conducted a covert operation inside the United States. If an intelligence operative from Israel gets arrested, so be it.'

'What about the Chinese? Will Shehadeh's pipeline go ahead?'

'The President supports the concept. If the Chinese build their base in the Sinai, he is going to get the Secretary of State to push to make sure the pipeline into Palestine happens.'

Senator Debra Donaldson returned to looking out of the window. In the distance, she could see clouds building. She reflected on the current situation in the world.

I feel a storm coming.

EPILOGUE

THE SINAI

Paul Shehadeh left the workers' camp in the Sinai and drove the Nissan Patrol east along the coast road. He wanted to check a potential border crossing site for his pipeline. A storm was forecast, but the morning sky was clear and bright. The cool morning desert surrounded him. It was his favourite time: before the sun monstered all living things. The low sunlight moved into the cracks and crevices of the rock and sand. Larger pieces of quartz in the shingle sparkled as the sun's rays rebounded from the crystals on the surface. The green, lush growth of New York State did not exist in this world, but the desert had a life of its own. The wind moved the sand and ate into the rocks, shaping the surrounding world.

He thought about his project to bring water to his people. China would build a desalination plant to justify their base in the Sinai. America, with the support of its allies, would pressure Israel to allow the pipeline to extend into the West Bank. Senator Debra Donaldson promised to speak to the President about it. She thought it could happen. He was happy. He was fulfilling his dream.

He stopped at the Egyptian checkpoint at Salah a-Din Gate. It took thirty minutes to get his special approval stamped and his vehicle waved forward. He drove on and stopped again at the Palestinian checkpoint at the other side of the buffer zone. The soldier looked at his papers, recognised him and waved him through. 'Allah maak,' said the guard wishing him well. Paul returned a smile and drove forward.

After clearing the buffer zone, he turned left onto the dirt road which ran alongside the metal wall that grew from the ground and reached into the sky. The wall split the land and separated Egypt from Gaza. He drove towards the coast searching for the site he believed would be suitable for his water pipeline to cross the border.

As he drove north towards the coast, a beam of electromagnetic radiation touched and stayed on his vehicle. At the same time, a General Dynamics F16 fighter flew towards him from the sea. The pilot reported that his weapons system had locked onto the beam of radiation.

'Target acquired,' reported the pilot.

'Fire when ready.'

Other books by Bob O'Brien:

Young Blood: The Story of the Family Murders
(2002)

*Water Barons: Money, politics
and control of water in Australia*
(2021)

www.ingramcontent.com/pod-product-compliance
Lightning Source LLC
Chambersburg PA
CBHW030606120726
47904CB00006B/1788